BEYOND DON

ELLY DANICA

BEYOND

Dreaming Past the Dark

DON'T

gynergy
books

Edited by: Jane Billinghurst
Cover illustration: Janet Riopelle
Printed and bound in Canada by: Best Book Manufacturers

gynergy books acknowledges the generous support of the Canada Council.

Published by:
gynergy books
P.O. Box 2023
Charlottetown, P.E.I.
Canada, C1A 7N7

Canadian Cataloguing in Publication Data

Danica, Elly, 1947-

Beyond don't

ISBN 0-921881-40-1

1. Danica, Elly, 1947- 2. Adult child sexual abuse victims. 3. Incest victims. I. Title.

HV6570.9.C3D34 1996   306.877'092   C96-950121-8

*This book is for Lucy, Ann,
Maria, Lila and Margie.*

Contents

Introduction

It is now ten years since I wrote the story of my childhood experiences, *Don't: A Woman's Word*. It has been an important decade in my life, and I decided to write about it in order to see more clearly the road I travelled during that time.

My life began in Holland, a couple of years after the end of the Second World War. In 1952 my parents moved to Canada with their five children, settling in Moose Jaw. I do not know precisely what precipitated this move, but it came swiftly after I first told my mother that my father had abused me. For the next fourteen years I lived in a household in hell as my father's violence and demands on me increased.

In the mid-1950s my father built a photography studio in the basement of the house. Soon he was hosting raucous evening parties in the basement, during which he photographed a series of nude "models" for the amusement of the men who were his "customers." As a child I was one of these models, and during one unforgettable night, when I was nine years old, I was photographed and then raped by a group of these men.

By the time I was fifteen, I had buried the horror of what was happening to me at home, acknowledging only that I had to get out of that house and as far away from my father as possible. It was clear that the only way I would be allowed to leave was if I married. I went in search of a young man who would treat me with respect, and I thought I had found him in the soldier I married at eighteen.

I left for Ontario with my husband the day after I married him. My marriage did not provide me with the release I had been hoping for. Five years later, when my son was born, I knew it was time to leave my husband, and possibly also my son. Something — I didn't understand what — brought me back to Saskatchewan. My plan was to go to university and try to build a better life than the one I had had until then.

I did not realize then that any step which brought me closer to acknowledging what had happened in my childhood would set off a series of nightmares and send me spiralling downward into pain and darkness. I had imagined that attending university in Regina would be as simple as taking classes, caring for my son and working toward a degree. Instead, alarm bells went off deep in my soul, and suddenly nothing was simple.

I had taken a daring first step toward adulthood and healing, but I had underestimated both how long it would take to get there and what I would have to come to terms with to make a better life possible. As my nightmares increased, I began to abuse drugs and alcohol. At the time I could not explain to myself or to anyone else why I was in so much pain, and so focused on either walking oblivion or suicide.

As the crisis that seemed to be my life deepened at university, I knew I would have to try something else and come back to work on a degree at a later time. I bought an old country church and settled in to write my way out of the mess I felt I was in. For the next thirteen years I struggled to understand the events of my childhood, even as I tried equally hard to deny that anything had happened to me.

Although in some ways it was incredibly difficult, writing the book that was to become *Don't* was the easy part: the manuscript was the culmination of more than ten years of keeping a journal, writing sometimes for as long as sixteen hours a day, just to sort out why there was so much pain and difficulty in my life. Eventually I had more than two thousand journal pages and a growing clarity about the issues.

In March 1987, in pain and terror, I finally wrote the story of my childhood. Then, in August, as a result of a chain reaction of serendipitous events, I found myself in Vancouver at West Word III, a school for women writers, in a workshop offered by Nicole Brossard. I left West Word ten days later with an offer to publish from Libby Oughton, then-publisher of gynergy books, and in May 1988 the book was launched. Once *Don't* was published, my life began to change in many ways.

After I finished the publicity tour for *Don't*, my life was somewhat better than it had been before the book was published. I had travelled the country, something I had always wanted to do. I had met and talked to a great many people. I had visited with my son for the first time in several years. Most important of all, I had been able to see my beloved grandmother in Holland before she died.

I was not, however, magically saved from the pain of my childhood, and I did not arrive at some mythical destination healed of all ills and sorrows. Yet there was a feeling that my journey ought to be over. *Don't* was selling well for a Canadian book, and I had appeared on many radio and television programs. Hot on the trail of success, a man showed up at my door, offering to help me invest my money. I laughed and said, "What money?" A couple of years later, another man came to my door, chanting my name like a mantra, apparently believing that only I had the power to convince social workers, the RCMP and television producers that he was not a sociopath. It is a myth of mass culture that having one's story taken up by television bestows such attendant blessings that one's life is forever set apart and one is "healed." It just isn't so. My real-life experiences did not guarantee salvation from poverty, and the burden of pain I carried remained grievous.

At first I was appalled by people's reactions to *Don't*. People hurt and cried reading what I had written, which made me feel wretched.

Instead of closing a chapter of my life, I was burdening others with it. For several years after the publication of *Don't*, whenever I went to the city and was recognized, I would be either stared at and whispered about, or approached by people who had horrific child-abuse disclosures they wished to share with me. I am not hard-hearted. I would listen and offer what comfort I could. But I found I could not get my errands done, attend workshops I had paid for or eat out as I had planned. I would arrive home exhausted, angry and confused. Eventually I stopped going out, and if I had to go to the library or grocery store, I would keep my head down, avoid meeting anyone's eyes and talk to nobody.

The problem was that I was no longer seen as a person separate and apart from the book. The sum total of my identity seemed to be the experience I had described. I began to feel erased by this unbearably narrow view of who I was. What about the rest of me? Growth, development, current projects, day-to-day issues or difficulties? None of it seemed to matter. By virtue of those ninety-six pages, I had become my childhood, period.

I wrote *Don't* to put the pain of my childhood behind me so that I could get on with the rest of my life. Instead, the book struck a chord with so many people that my childhood experience ruled my life in a new way. I gave interviews and speeches, responded to disclosures and talked about nothing else from the spring of 1988 until late in 1994. Although I enjoy public speaking immensely — the hermit happily admits she loves an audience — I found it increasingly difficult to find the energy to speak only about child abuse, because, despite giving what comfort and support I could to others, I was unable to find any for myself.

I have, throughout the course of readings, speeches and work-shops generated by the publication of *Don't*, been extremely ambivalent. What is my responsibility to this issue? I wonder. How do I meet whatever responsibility I identify, yet retain some semblance of a normal life? Am I entitled to my life as an artist, away from the work on child-abuse issues? Must I, because my book has touched so many people, continue to work in this field? Or can I allow myself a different sort of life?

These are some of the questions I have been wrestling with. I don't yet have clear answers. This book is an effort to find answers, or perhaps, by looking back at the experiences of the last several years, to find better questions. I see this project as a spiritual journey, a search for renewal and enlarged meaning in my life. I know that making an effort, any positive effort, helps take me in the right direction and helps build toward the changes in life and attitude that I seek.

O n e

Beginning
the Journey

Sorrow: for a long time I thought that sorrow was all I had. I thought that I would spend my whole life mourning what had been stolen from me: a peaceful and nurturing childhood; a sense of personal integrity; a healthy, positive identity; and self-worth.

I am the only one in my family of seven sisters and three brothers to have spoken out about the abuse that pervaded the household we grew up in. As a child, I had buried what I knew until I was aware of only hatred and constant pain. I could not understand why, as an adult, I abused myself with drugs, alcohol, relationships, anything that came my way and worked to anaesthetize me, for however short a time. Not until I had written the story of my childhood was I able to name my pain.

Several lifetimes of keening and weeping could not express my sorrow. It is boundless and will resound, with my accusations, into eternity. And from its depths, I say: I have been terribly betrayed.

From this profound sense of betrayal, I had to find my way to health, well-being and understanding, and to do that I had to learn to mourn what I had lost. I began to write to understand my feelings, and most particularly my deep sadness. I knew there was pain, but I wasn't ready to acknowledge where it came from. At the beginning I was not aware that I was writing a book. It made me feel better to write, so I wrote.

I began to keep a journal. I can't recommend this enough for anyone in the process of recovery from abuse. Writing a journal gives you a sense of the progress you have made. It can be read as travelogue, for even on the trip to hell and back we need to know where we have been and what we are putting behind us. Some women who prefer pictures to words have kept their journals in images or doodles, and this is also a powerful technique.

I find that sitting quietly with a pen in hand to describe my progress through a day encourages access to the past. When I wrote about my memories, they felt grounded, and I could begin to look at them. The more I examined them, the more I was able to understand them. In the beginning, understanding was all I sought. The pain was not noticeably less the first time I wrote of it, but I often found a new way to look at it, one that brought with it a small but growing sense of release from the powerful grip it had on my life. It took many years, however, before I was aware of my change in perspective.

I find out about that change by looking back in my journal and measuring the distance from my old self to my present one. Every day the distance is greater, for as I write about the past, I create, word by word, breath by breath, a new reality. In those early days of my recovery process, reading about where I had been gave me the courage to go on, for there was always one more memory to look at and, for a while, always one more horror to face.

One of my deep sorrows is that I will never forget what I have endured. My journal has helped me reach the stage where I no longer think it a useful goal to forget something that was so much a part of my life. My progress feels wonderful, and I no longer spend my days so entirely absorbed by my memories. There is some ease now; the pain is not so acute, nor is it my only reality.

I did think of suicide, but most of the time I knew that what I really wanted was an end to the pain, not to my life. In my day-to-day reality, I was continuously assured by doctors I consulted and by my husband, while I was with him, that my pain was imaginary, even when my body proved the existence of my pain by exhibiting a series of what were called, for twenty years, psychosomatic illnesses.

The first thing I learned, in a long list of strategies to survive my childhood, was not to trust anybody. The second thing I learned was not to trust myself. This is the sorrow I most want to heal, and the one with which I seem to have made the greatest progress in the last few years.

When you don't trust yourself, you learn to hide the truth. From an early age, I realized that the truth about what was happening was extremely dangerous to me. I began to find ways to get around the truth — to learn, as the poet says, to tell it with a slant. This was difficult because I was young and because I didn't want to have to lie. But neither did I want to create the kind of conflict that my first effort to tell the truth about the abuse had triggered. When I had aired that truth, my family had ended up moving to another continent. So, in order to tell others what I thought they wanted to hear, I had to learn to lie to myself.

I learned to ignore how I really felt and to feel as I was told I ought to feel. I began to live on two levels: the level of responding to the abusers', my mother's and my teachers' expectations; and the level of my denied inner life. I soon found I was happier if I did not acknowledge that inner life, and I abandoned it in favour of the image that other people wanted of me — of a devout and obedient Catholic child — which seemed so much safer. And that is how I learned to split my personality. And that is also why, well into my thirties, I had no idea who I was or what I really thought or felt about anything. Except for one thing: I was madder than hell about something, but having learned to be a good girl, I usually kept this well hidden. Or so I thought.

It is a strange paradox that the ability to dissociate and split is one of the most important survival techniques I developed as a child, and that it then proved to be one of the most difficult things to let go of and overcome as an adult, when I began the work of healing. Of course it was hard to let this go — for was it not what had kept me alive? How could I survive without this split, which so conveniently kept the pain at a distance, at least sometimes? But I learned slowly, so very slowly, to feel safe, and then I found I no longer needed to dissociate, leave my body, fragment, hide.

As I began the work of healing, I remember kicking and screaming, wishing the work were over, always. I do not have patience with the process of recovery, even when I take such pains to document my progress day by day. My progress always feels too slow, far too slow! Now I realize that the process went as quickly as I could cope with it, and I believe this is true for everyone. We make progress when we are ready, not before. If we are not ready when we think we ought to be, it is better to re-examine our expectations than to indulge in self-hate because we are not meeting an agenda that may not even be our own. There is a personal sense that we ought to "get over it"; therapists, a spouse, friends and society generally seem to demand that we get on with our lives and come to terms with the past in as short a time as possible.

My recovery process limped along from crisis to crisis. For months I was not aware of making any progress at all, and then a new crisis would erupt in my life. Gradually I learned that a crisis signalled that I had been making progress after all, and that I was now getting too close to uncovering a memory that I was not yet ready to acknowledge. The crisis, which I had often brought upon myself, diverted my attention from the recovery process by giving me something else on which to focus.

Part of my problem with healing is that I try to build mountains without moving or touching pebbles or rocks. Here I was, trying to will the mountains of my well-being into existence because I could imagine them — see them clearly in all their massy splendour. But I did not want to get out the wheelbarrow and start moving the dirt or handling the stones that were my past and the terror I felt about it. There was something missing from my vision of the result — how to get there. I was so impatient to put the pain behind me that

I did not want to take the time to go through my memories one by one. I did not want to write them all down and look at each in turn. After each new memory surfaced, I wanted to say, "This is enough. I know all I need to know about my past and I can go forward from here."

My visions were grand. I saw myself in seven-league boots; in three giant leaps I intended to be at my goal of being well and happy. I felt grand visions could be achieved only by magical and instantaneous means, and not by the painstaking tracking of memories long hidden from view. I tried now and then to concentrate on a stone, or even a grain of sand. Then another crisis would loom, and I would lose focus. It took me a long time to realize that if I was to reach my goal, I could not escape the gruelling work of examining my past in detail. I also could not allow recurring crises to distract me from my healing work.

I found it was easier to accept the work that had to be done if I compared my inner struggle to a physical challenge. If you plan to climb a mountain, you undergo a training period before you begin (awareness of the issues you are facing), and you start with easy, short climbs (a slow letting-go of denial and negative behaviours) with experienced guides (sharing experiences with others). You outfit yourself with harness, ropes, pick, helmet and companions, whatever will keep you safe and enable you to make progress. Continuing this metaphor, I find comfort in the image of the Goddess of the Mountain as a guide for this climb.

You climb only one mountain at a time, not the whole chain in one leap. You don't really see much of the world with seven-league boots — everything goes by too fast — and that usually means you will have to retrace your steps. Each mountain requires different skills, but one thing is certain — climbing becomes easier with experience and practice. And it will always be a good workout. The journey is at least as important as the destination, though I lose sight of that almost as often as I blink my eyes or draw breath.

As I was going through my process of recovery, I needed to remind myself that the work I was doing was vitally necessary, and I needed to have the courage to trust as it affected my life. I had trouble accepting the process because it took time, and because it could not be manipulated by intellectual effort, no matter how much energy I expended. I could not speed the process up when I thought it ought to go faster. I could not leap from phase to phase simply because I lacked patience or had become too uncomfortable with where I was.

I recognize now that I slowed things down when I tried to meddle with the healing process. For instance, if the work I was doing became too intense, or the progress I was making frightened me, I became intensely involved in a relationship chosen only for its distraction value; or I went on eating or drinking binges; or I ran away from home — anything at all disruptive that was sure to lead me on an extended detour from my healing path. Inevitably, I found I had to give up what was usually a negative activity and return to my work of recovery.

The best way for me to keep track of my progress is to look back and see how far I have come. This is why I keep a journal. When I know where I have been, I feel less anxiety about my current struggles and difficulties. I am also more understanding of what I perceive at the time to be my failures, for by looking back I can see that what seemed to be failure at the time often leads to progress, or to an important lesson in the end. This was particularly clear when I went on allergy-food binges, just to feel terrible and distracted. At these times I would feel that I had broken faith with myself, when what I really needed was a rest from the intensity of the work I was doing — a rest I did not know how to grant myself.

I use my journal to remind me of the importance of always moving forward in the healing process, for if I stray from the path, I find myself investing in stasis, which is unattainable except in depression, psychosis or death. This does not mean that I do not get stuck for long periods; it means the price of staying stuck is a heavy one indeed.

I try to deny the demands of the healing process because the models I have been given are those of life-denying perfectionism: I was rigorously trained in the 1950s by parents, nuns and Catholicism to be an always smiling, polite, self-effacing, obedient breeder.

In the model handed down to me, women were not expected to grow as human beings, to experience any spiritual development or change in their lives, from child to adolescent through to young married woman, mother, middle age, old age. We were required to have the same silly smiles on our faces, the same submissive attitudes, whether we were three or ninety-three. To me it seemed that nothing about our lives mattered. What mattered was that men were pleased with our performance and suffered no physical or emotional discomfort from our particular reality; what mattered was that children appeared but did not become troublesome little persons with lives and needs of their own; what mattered most of all was that women not burden men or society with what they perceived as our messy bodies and our even messier, diffuse and illogical minds.

I grew up thinking that weak women were subject to physical processes such as menstruation and pregnancy, which they could not control and were required to deny and hide. Males, who I thought were strong and definitely got to do what they wanted in the world, lived their lives entirely beyond physical processes. It was a simplistic view, yes, but when I was young and untaught, this is what I believed. Puberty brought monthly indications of my female process. Not me, I said, by the third period, not me! I don't want to live chained to this. I want a different choice. I want a female process-free life — a lovely, naïve contradiction. I want the same freedom from process that I think I see in the lives of my father and brothers. Physical female process, as I saw it then, was always negative, left me ever more powerless and brought too much pain.

When I was a child, denial became a way of life. At school — if I wanted to get home without being waylaid by bullies and beaten up for my difference — I was required to deny that I had been born in Holland, spoke Dutch as my first language and was an immigrant. At home, denial was how I learned to see the abuse I endured as normal or inevitable. Allowing myself to see only the relatively safe aspects of the abuse — that is, the beatings I got and the food that was withheld — I would not have to see farther, to the sexual abuse.

As a teen I hated my father, yes, but that was much safer than acknowledging why I hated him.

Denial is one of the most difficult hurdles of all. It's clever. It goes underground. You can play-act that you have overcome it, for it is so strong and cunning that it has enormous energy for deceit at its disposal. But as you play-act, you learn; and what you learn is how to banish denial, one tiny step at a time. The energy that comes with denial is the means to finally overcoming it. Eventually I came to the place where I could no longer swim through such thick muck, and I wanted to use the energy this takes, denial's energy, to feel better, to take charge of my life.

There is only one sure way to free the energy, and that is to let go of denial. But there is enormous pain involved in letting go. I felt that I could not cope with more pain; that I did not yet have the quality of trust that would let me believe that letting go meant I would feel better, really feel better. I would run up to letting go and pull back. Letting go of denial appeared to me as an abyss, and all I could see was its edge. Though I was convinced I knew how deep the pit beyond must be, I didn't really believe in freedom from the pain I carried. I thought that if I had a closer look at what was going on in my life, I would drop into a blacker pit than the one I had begun to crawl out of. And I said to myself that I wasn't that foolish, no longer that easily suckered.

There came a day, though, when I had no other desirable choice: I was faced with the realization that I must make the leap of faith that would take me beyond denial, the first step in regaining health and a sense of personal integrity — for how could either be possible as long as I continued to lie to myself about what had really happened to me?

I took the leap of faith, and suddenly I knew why I was doing it, and that it was worth the enormous effort it demanded of me. I glimpsed a brighter future. It wasn't much at that moment, but it was a start. Now I had something to work toward. And in the days that followed this epiphany, the energy that had supported the denial was slowly freed to help me make the commitment to deepen my healing work.

I believe that denial worked, initially, to keep me safe until I was strong enough to cope with what burdened me, until I had a safe place in which to begin to look at my pain, until I could find the help and support I needed for the journey. This is not to say that it is positive or necessary to hang on to denial beyond its time. However, what you see as my denial, or I see as yours, may be all that holds us together. Since you cannot know precisely my healing process, nor I yours, neither of us has the right to confront the other with what we perceive to be denial, demanding instantaneous change. Instead it's best to be non-judgmental and supportive, trusting that each of us will take the leap of faith as soon she is able, and knowing that none of us can save another from herself. Only I can take responsibility for myself, see myself as I really am, when I'm ready, and then walk beyond denial into the light.

An awakening took place when I let go of denial. I felt reborn, and began to learn to stand upright, taking up space in and with my own body. I began to learn to speak authentically as my true self. I finally saw the spiral path, saw that it had widened, that more light shone upon it. Yet some things I had to do again and again until I had the lessons clear: struggles with ambivalent feelings for both my parents, with siblings, with lovers, with responsibility for my son and, especially, ongoing struggles with all the residuals of the abuse in my life.

Letting go of denial allowed me, at last, to begin to see clearly. I learned to name my experience truthfully, for the first time, without euphemism or minimizing, without the language that protects the abusers and erases me. Instead of merely saying that I had had a rotten childhood, I was able to acknowledge that I had been physically and emotionally abused, raped and pimped by my father. I heard clearly now things I had never let myself hear before, such as verbal abuse, and I began to name that too.

Just as a person whose vision and hearing are restored after blindness and deafness is completely overwhelmed for a while, so was I overwhelmed. And my first reaction was to retreat, seemingly to go backwards into the denial again. But it was not possible, and deep down I knew that. All I really needed was to rest for a time before I continued with the healing. This was my life's hardest work, after all.

I manufactured many a crisis in my life because I knew of no other way to have time out. I wasn't yet at a place in my recovery where I could simply state that I needed a respite, even to myself. I felt things moved too fast, and I was terrified of movement. Mind you, I walked this path alone, without therapists, support groups, or even books to comfort me.

For me the healing process consisted of ten years of approach-avoidance manoeuvres. I'd work hard to chisel a path so I could approach the issues, and then I'd run like hell as soon as I made the slightest progress forward. The saying "One step forward, three steps back" for me meant one step forward, three kilometres back.

During this time I had a little car. Each morning, as soon as I got up, I would drive 100 kilometres to the nearest city for coffee and then drive home. I didn't seem to live anywhere; I was always in transit. I simply found comfort in driving that same stretch of road, over and over. I put 100,000 kilometres on my car in less than two years. The point is that, even running or driving in what I thought of as the opposite direction (though of course it was not), I still made snail's progress, and eventually I could no longer sustain the effort it took to do so much running or driving.

Yet it still took a major crisis for me to find the courage to make significant changes in my life. A massive tumour on an ovary was discovered during a routine medical examination. (Was everything that I held onto so strenuously collected into one lump, so I would finally have to give it some attention?) Doctors treated the situation as a high priority, booking surgery within days. It might be cancer, they whispered. I went into instant denial. I broke appointments, refused several times to show up at the hospital for surgery, refused to take any advice from alarmed doctors.

I was cornered and I knew it. Denial helped me buy time to think it through. Eventually I realized that I felt out of control, and then why I felt this way. The surgeon I had seen gave me the creeps. He was grossly insulting and reminded me of the abusers; I could not face the idea of being treated by him while I was unconscious.

I knew I needed to find a surgeon I could trust, and as soon as I made an appointment with a different one, much of my terror and denial dispersed. I still had to face surgery, I still postponed it so that I could go to the opening of my first one-woman painting exhibition, but I knew I had made the commitment to take care of myself and to get the help I needed.

This crisis brought the child abuse much closer to the surface. I knew it was time I looked at what was really wrong with my life. I began to realize that, just as I risked an early death by denying the tumour, I might equally risk untimely death by continuing to deny my past and the grievous pain it still caused. I could not face it yet, but I made a commitment to do so — which was the first step. I stopped denying there was a problem, even if I could not yet cope with looking at what the problem was.

I was then thirty-nine years old, and I was finding it more and more difficult to get by in the world at the emotional age of nine. It was a great relief to stop pretending I was just fine. Surgery found the tumour to be benign. I was glad I had trusted, and paid attention to, my reaction to the first surgeon, and was grateful for the skill of the second one. I mended well.

That spring I got my first computer. A friend who had seen me through an earlier surgery, and had been appalled by how long I took to recover from it, felt that I needed a new interest in my life and that perhaps a computer would help me finally write that book I had been talking about. I enjoyed playing with the computer, and by the fall I decided that I was ready to attempt the fiction project I had been making notes for and planning for some time. I worked flat out for two and a half months. As I did, I thought how much better this all was than trying to come to terms with my own past. What I wanted to write was fiction about other women's pasts, not mine.

Of course it didn't work. The writing project died. I sank into yet another wretched depression, and stayed there until I went back to read my journal of the spring and was reminded of the commitment I had made. I saw a glimmer of light, and I wrote my way to that point. Ten years of filling more than two thousand pages with my dances toward it and screaming retreats left me with the image of a tunnel in a mountain. Once I got out of the tunnel, I knew I would have to climb the mountain. I did not think I could do that. I had no help, no guide, no one to hold my hand so I could take the first steps. So I wrote, creating a rope ladder, learning to climb one word, one day, at a time.

There were things I recognized early in this part of my recovery process. I knew I was filled with hatred, but I had not yet let myself know why. I knew I was potentially dangerous to my son and definitely dangerous to myself. What I failed to allow myself to see (for what could I have done with the knowledge?) was that this was all very serious indeed. The doctors I saw throughout my teens and twenties — for my hate? — prescribed Valium. I learned to mix it with beer and gin, and thereby to at least double the pain relief. I had a huge investment in oblivion.

This is the part of recovery where I was most in danger of losing myself. It is so easy to go over the edge or get stuck here — body processes take over, and before you know it you are physically addicted to whatever you have been using to try to keep numbness between you and the pain, or even just between you and the recognition that there is a problem. I used many things other than prescription drugs and alcohol in an addictive manner — religion, food, relationships — anything that could build a sea wall between me and my pain.

It takes enormous energy to keep from recognizing that a problem exists. And that's what ultimately brought everything crashing down around me. For me, a medical crisis was the last straw. Other women have said that it doesn't have to be a major crisis, though it is always a personally significant one. Some women speak of crises brought on by the death of a parent, whether the offender or not, or by the birth of a child. For others, it is anything that causes upheaval: losing a relationship or beginning one, changing jobs, moving houses, or even achieving some long-cherished goal. When you are hanging on by your fingertips, it doesn't take much to unbalance your life.

So one day there was a flash of light. I saw the tunnel exit and realized I would have to do something now or die before my time.

Like hell, I said, and denial began with a vengeance. The tunnel exit disappeared. My sense that there was a problem was quashed under the weight of my fear. I threw myself fiercely into a new relationship or a new project. No way was I going to leave the nice safe tunnel I had lived in for so long and climb a mountain — for who would I be then?

And the new relationship, the many projects, the things I thought would make me happy, became dust and ashes. The hole where my self and heart should have been was boundless. I felt so very, very empty, and then I found the word "void" in the dictionary, and I thought it might be my name.

If somebody had told me then that my denial had created the void, I would not have believed it. How could accepting that I had been abused fill this void with so much as the breath of one atom? Ah, but not only the pain, the abuse and the hatred had been denied, but also my growth, health, life and energy: everything I thought would never be mine because some twist of fate had brought me into the world carrying a great cosmic emptiness instead of a heart and soul.

If you deny that you hate, you leave no room for love to grow. If you deny your pain, you lock out joy. If you deny your dis-ease, you cannot achieve ease and health. If you deny what was destroyed in your childhood, you cannot know the fullness of life as an adult. If you deny, then all the parts of self and soul are blocked and you cannot release the energy needed to do the healing work. It carries a huge price tag, this denial.

Denial had been a way of life for me for so long that I should have known it was rooted firmly somewhere. And so it was. Denial enveloped recognition of the problem; it both preceded and followed it. For as long as I denied the need for the healing process, I didn't have to give up my feelings of being a victim or take adult responsibility for myself. As long as I was in denial, I did not have to take care of myself, but in not taking care of myself, I also could not acknowledge strength, growth or, in fact, anything positive.

As long as there was this denial in the way, I did not have much access, if any, to a positive and healthy future. It was almost as though denial was saying, "Well, I can't deny what happened any more, but I can deny you the vision to see it clearly, deny you the insight to see your strengths and hope." Eventually I realized that I could not be fooled by this. Not any more. This was the same old denial thinking I wouldn't recognize it for what it was. The question now was: Could I find the courage to see clearly enough to acknowledge both the necessity of the healing process and the strength I most certainly possessed to engage with it?

The process of recovery: a journey from here to there; a quest for a healthy, whole self; for contentment; for a sure sense of my life's path; learning of the work to be done and beginning it; being as sure as one can be, with at least some idea of a plan.

The best news, once we have taken the phenomenal leap of faith out of denial, is that we are now involved in a process that will make positive changes in our lives. This is both comforting and as frustrating as can be. If there is one thing we do not want to hear, it is that this all takes time. I woke from the long sleep of denial ready to tackle anything — mountain climbing, space walks, anything — as long as I could get it done in the next thirty-six hours.

If someone had presented me then with a list of the aspects of the recovery process that I would encounter, in my impatience to be done with it all, I probably would have dismissed it out of hand as not applying to me. I had carried all this stuff for over thirty years. The last thing I wanted to hear was that now I needed to focus more time, more energy and more thought on the process of coming to terms with it. I wanted to hear that I would feel better, magically, tomorrow.

I think the biggest single thing I learned in 1986, the year I finally began to let go of denial, was that none of the abuse I endured as a child was my fault. What a revelation! Just waking up in the morning was easier after that. I began, finally, to shed the burden of guilt. And now every step I took forward showed me real progress. I no longer felt I was going backwards — well, at least not most days.

There were still plenty of things I could not face, often simple things that just seemed to be more than I could manage. If I looked long enough at the task that threatened to overwhelm me, asked enough times, "Why is this?", I eventually came face to face with the fear behind my inability to embark on it. Once I saw what was really going on, I could decide whether I felt strong enough to tackle the task or whether I needed to leave it for another day. I was beginning to make choices based on how I felt, rather than reacting to what I thought I ought to be doing. Chalk up another big step!

I wish I could say there was an easier path to recovery than facing all the horrors of the past. I wish I could say there were shortcuts. All I can report are rest stops along the way, and detours that are more or less dangerous, depending on what they are. Though the detours can significantly lengthen the process, we come back to the same path eventually.

Once each horror has been faced and we have shed all those tears, the past begins to lose its power over us. I used to ask, "How do I know when I've really faced something, not just played clever games with myself about it?" The answer to this question seemed ridiculous to me then, but now I understand something of its wisdom: When you have truly faced something, your behaviour changes and you begin to have more energy.

I did not see the positive side of this for a long time, for the first behaviour changes seemed to me to be for the worse. Where I once had only occasional nightmares, now they appeared several times a week, leaving me reeling and stunned by their power and violence. For a while I lost the boundaries between nightmares and the waking world. The nightmares were so real that my entire life seemed to be caught up in them.

I began the process of writing the book that was to become *Don't* by asking myself this question: How did I get here? My immediate response was: slowly. I got here much too slowly, for I could imagine aspects of a different, healthier and happier life more than thirty years ago.

From the time I was four years old until I left his house fourteen years later, my father, depending on his mood, raped, beat or starved me, unhindered by anything except my stubborn will to survive. This man moved through life from one vicious whim or fantasy to the next. Eventually he developed the abuse of me and my sisters into a lucrative business, selling the use of his daughters and photographs of our humiliation to men in the community. Apparently, he has now retired in considerable comfort on the proceeds. I am the only one of seven daughters who has accused him. My five surviving sisters continue to deny the horror we endured in lieu of our childhoods, for to them it seems quite normal.

As a child, there never was a time I didn't fight him, didn't know he was wrong or didn't hate him for what he did. I am, I think, lucky in this: My grandmother (my mother's mother) supported me, believed me absolutely, when I told her about the first time he abused me, when I was four years old. She assured me that she and my grandfather had talked to him, that he would never do anything like that again. Of course, this was not to be, but even so, I knew that she had tried to stop him and, more important, that what he had done to me was wrong. If I had not known this, had not had the memory of a grandmother who I knew loved me, but whom I did not see again until thirty-eight years later, I do not think I would have survived. Too much was against me, too much effort was made to break and destroy me.

I clung to a dream vision of my grandmother in Holland all through my childhood: I talked to her by asking the moon to take her my messages and by talking to the little Hummel figurine of the Madonna and child she sent me for my first communion. The moon, the figurine and my grandmother were all muddled in my mind, so that I prayed to all of them for help and protection from my father. There was no point asking my mother for either, since she had assured me there was nothing she could do. She had six, then seven, eight, nine other kids to feed, and told me that what my father wanted was a price that must be paid. I had no choice, she said, and neither did she.

My mother made the sort of concessions to our captor that are now better understood in terms of the hostage syndrome and battered-wife behaviour. She made what she felt were small sacrifices (me, my health, my safety, my childhood) to protect both herself and her younger children. She knew, she said, that I was strong, knew I could take it, knew I would be all right. She may well have been right about my strength, but she was definitely wrong that I ought to have been sacrificed to keep him from hurting the others. She was wrong in thinking that he would be satisfied with only one of her daughters, when there were so many more. Slowly, surely, he preyed on the others. Each time she said, Well, that one, but none of the rest. Her final effort, to protect her youngest daughter, failed too. By then she had nothing left with which to bargain.

I don't imagine my mother ever saw or acknowledged the pattern he so clearly followed with her children. She did not ever think she could stop him, or even demand that he stop. I see her failure to protect us as the result of a long attrition of her will and spirit: he blackmailed, bribed, threatened and occasionally beat her. He broke her as surely as he broke me. She saw no hope, said we would starve without him, knew she was trapped and tried to make the best of it. My mother never sought help or fought back. She was an immigrant woman with ten kids; this was her problem and she had no choice but to deal with it alone.

From the time I first heard about the plans to move us all to Canada — away from the so-called meddling of my grandmother — I thought only of getting away from my father. Like someone in prison, I counted down the years, months and days until I would be free. It proved to be not nearly as easy as my child mind thought it would be. And when I finally left home at eighteen, I most certainly was not free of him simply because I no longer lived in his house.

❖ ❖ ❖

For years I was the classic little mother, carrying the burdens of a household of twelve people that my mother was no longer required to manage. It tired her too much, and then she was not available to wait on him or to help him entertain the customers, so she was forbidden by him to do any housework, and I was obliged to do it all. I was thirteen years old and five feet two of resentment and weariness. In the basement, at night, business was booming.

Some time in my fifteenth year, my father tried to strangle me so as to be forever rid of the accusation I could not keep from my eyes. My mother, in her one effort to protect me from him, pulled his hands away from my throat, but screamed at me as she did so, accusing me of willfulness and of upsetting him. I fell from his grasp like a stone and still cannot understand why she waited such an eternity to stop him.

I can see them both standing there in the kitchen, infuriated at me, both blaming me for what he did. I remember looking at them and knowing, finally, that I was broken. I had nothing left to fight him with. I don't think I had taken his threats seriously until then. I realized that I would have to learn to be more careful, much more careful, if I was going to survive. I did not know if there was help anywhere, certainly had never heard of any and probably wouldn't have believed in it, so escape was not an option. What I did believe, because I knew it by then, was that he could kill me any time he chose to exert himself, and that maybe there would be somebody there to stop him, and maybe not.

I became a robot. He'd snap his fingers and bark an order at me, demand I do a task, and I'd perform without speaking or thinking. I made my face into a mask, which my father always swore was a sneer. Occasionally he'd beat me just for the hell of it, because he enjoyed hurting me, saying he'd change the mask I wore, even if he killed me in the effort; but I bore that too, without weeping, crawling away afterwards to finish the dishes or to iron his two white shirts for the next day.

For nearly twenty-five years I kept my memory, my feelings, almost my very being, shut down, because some part of me knew it was the only way to survive. Somewhere along the road I lost the reasons for my denial. Eventually I didn't remember any other way of being in the world. Didn't remember a time when I'd lived in my body, instead of beside or above it. Didn't remember what it was to have any feeling other than terror. Didn't think it odd that I remembered almost nothing before my marriage at eighteen. Didn't even think it odd that I hated my father — for no apparent or remembered reason.

I became a very good actor. I'd watch people and mimic whatever behaviours or emotional responses I thought appropriate to the occasion or event in my life. I developed a veritable repertoire of feelings and reactions. I was so good at this that I fooled myself into thinking it was normal. Of course, I couldn't explain to myself the night terrors, the days of weeping, the physical and emotional paralysis or the multitude of fears and phobias I acquired. As time went on, I had to work ever harder to keep myself from remembering. Every time there was a crisis, I'd develop another bizarre coping skill. And I withdrew farther and farther into myself.

Twenty-five years ago I packed up the last of my household goods in an army officer's bungalow in Petawawa, Ontario. That May, I hoisted my nine-month-old son into a childcarrier on my back, and together he and I boarded a train bound for Regina. I had convinced my husband to resign from the military so that I could get away from the idiocy of military life. I had been married for six years, I was twenty-four and I was certain only of one thing: that the stifling, intensely macho and violent atmosphere of military life was not healthy for me or my child.

That was what I could talk to my husband about, but I had another, hidden agenda. This leaving for Regina was the first step I took toward leaving my husband. The rest of the dream I had sometimes tried to share with him: I wanted a place in the country, a writing life, other artistic endeavours. He always had the same response: he found my pretensions to a life of my own stupid and funny.

The first thing I did when I arrived in Regina was to sign up for a university course. I was accepted as a "mature student," because I had never finished high school, and I began classes in the fall of 1971. I wanted to realize my dream of becoming an archaeologist and a writer. I had both a passion for and an incredible fear of creative writing. As I did not yet feel safe enough to embark on my writing career, I wanted to get an education suitable for the writer I wished to become.

A year into my classes, I left my son with my husband and moved into a one-room apartment furnished with a mattress and a bookcase. I was going to get a degree and then become a writer, I said, each time my husband asked me what the hell I was doing and when I was coming home. When I left my husband and my child, I realized that it was becoming more and more difficult to keep myself together with gum and sticky tape. I was out of my marriage, but I did not know where I was going.

My lack of a life plan heightened the almost overwhelming sense of insecurity from which I suffered. On the surface I was doing something I wanted to do — attending university — but below the surface I felt intense guilt and fear of punishment. I now realize that these negative feelings resurface whenever I do anything for myself, and I have to be constantly on my guard against them. By the spring of my third year at university, I knew that I was losing it, for I spent most weekends in a haze of alcohol and Valium, planning my death.

At the time, I had no clear idea of what I had stepped into or why I was suddenly awash in terror and pain. I did not know why I felt I was drowning in something I could not see or describe. Valium and alcohol deadened everything, and as long as I could indulge in them in sufficient quantities, I didn't have nightmares. Mind you, my daytime reality had as much of a nightmare quality as my dreams.

I tried over and over, but I still could not begin to write what I thought of as my "real work." Not a single word could be coaxed onto paper. I could not define what this "real work" was, but I had a sense I would know it when I saw it. In the meantime, I could not even write a simple essay for a university class. Writing for myself, which I had told myself was the reason I had left my husband and my son, was now the last thing on earth I could do. I was terrified of what the words would say, what I would have to acknowledge if I told myself even the tiniest bit of the truth. And I knew that if I opened the floodgates, even the width of an eyelash, I would drown in the pain. There was only one thing to do, I thought, and that was never to let the smallest bit surface, to keep it all dammed up behind the pathetic façade I presented to the world.

So when the urge to write became irresistibly insistent, I did what I had done in the first few months of my wretched marriage: I wrote letters to my sisters in which I told every species of lie about my life, creating a fiction of myself, for I was their oldest sister, the only one to have aspirations of a university degree and a career, and

I had, I thought, a responsibility to show them my successful self, trotting out an adulthood I possessed only on paper. Perhaps the best fiction I have yet written was in those letters sent back to the little sisters I missed so much.

What I didn't tell them was that by now I weighed just over thirty-six kilograms and was given to alcohol and Valium binges; that I ate only a couple of times a week and was so malnourished I was losing my hair in clumps, and my teeth shifted in my mouth with every movement of my jaw. I could not explain why, when I was doing something that I had always wanted to do, I was so desperately unhappy.

The anxiety level I lived with was unbearable without Valium. The doctors never questioned my need for the drug. They just gave me ever-stronger prescriptions, and instructions to take the drug more often. I was a twenty-six-year-old basket case, in the doctor's office every couple of weeks, and spending most of my time trying to figure out a nice, painless way to die. No one, ever, asked me why.

It was a bleak and wretched time — and it would have been substantially relieved had I been able to write a little truth now and then. I know now that I was terrified of what I would have to face if I was honest with myself, and that the only way to avoid this confrontation was to stay stoned and drunk and away from writing anything more demanding than letters to my sisters.

I wonder what I could have done, what ease there might have been for my suffering, if I could have found a way to tell someone what I thought this pain was all about, I tried to talk to friends, anyone who would listen for an hour. But it was easy to see that my fierce hatred and rage quickly became too much for any of them to deal with. I could not shut it off and be sociable. I was terrible company.

Sometime in the summer of 1974, I surfaced long enough to think about what I wanted to do, what I had better do if I was going to make it to my thirtieth birthday. What I wanted more than anything was to feel better, but I had no idea how to feel, so "better" was a dream more distant than anything I could imagine. I decided that since my life was a disaster anyway, I might as well pick up where I had left off five years earlier and get serious about weaving and spinning. University classes were impossible by then. I was not able to cope with any demands, even the simplest. I was no longer able to get up in the morning if I knew I was required to do something. But if left alone, I could putter with yarns and weave or spin for a couple of hours and get through another day.

In January 1975, over the phone and for $300, I bought an old church in rural Saskatchewan. It was essentially a barn without windows, having been abandoned to the elements and village juveniles five years previously. I knew instinctively that it was time for me to burrow and find out what was wrong, what was so desperately wrong, with me. It was not an option to go for help. I knew from experience there wasn't any. Sure there were psychiatrists, and drugs to make you slow and stupid, but there wasn't anything like help or understanding. If I was going to do it, if I was going to survive, I would have to figure out how to do it myself.

I couldn't do what I needed to in the city. If I was going to change my life, I had to get away from the temptations of the bar scenes and from the stresses of city life. I needed an existence that made no demands on me other than getting through the next twenty-four hours. Moving to the country, into a drafty barn of a building with no windows, heat, electricity or plumbing, and me with no income other than a couple more months of unemployment insurance, brought day-to-day survival into the foreground in a way I had not expected. Since I had only a vague perception of reality, I had no idea what I expected to live on or how I would get through the winter. Cope? Hah! I was out of my depth the minute I walked a step out of the city. I had never lived without plumbing or cooked on a wood stove. Wood had to be split before I could have a cup of coffee! I knew I'd gone off the deep end, but, as I said to myself and the few horrified friends who drove out from the city to see what I was up to: You see, I can write here.

The official move into the old church took place in January 1976, during a blizzard on New Year's weekend. Plastic covered the broken windows. The building was so cold that I slept in long-johns, hat, parka, ski pants and mitts, buried under every scrap of blanket and coat I owned. Every morning I would get up and stoke the wood stove to bring the temperature up to just above freezing. I was miserably poor, cold and hungry, yet I felt so much better than I had in the city. I was still in pain, still having horrible nightmares, but I knew I was finally on the right track.

I began my long, slow healing process through my hands. It made me feel good (and slightly warmer) to be absorbed completely in a weaving project. I taught myself and was soon very skilled at it, eventually winning prizes for work that would culminate, ten years later, in a gallery showing of my textiles. Poverty, however, seemed never-ending, for although people praised my work, it never found a steady market, though I hauled mountains of scarves, stoles, jackets, ponchos and rugs to craft fairs and tried to sell them through the trendy little craft shops of the time.

I cannot adequately describe how important the work with my hands was to my healing. Even as I felt ugly and hopeless beyond measure, my hands learned to speak an eloquent beauty and to weave the strands of my future into whole cloth. I could not see the beauty I made, fought seeing it for many years. Yet I now see how vital this work with my hands was to my process of recovery.

But I did not only sit at a loom or spinning-wheel, trying to earn a living with my hands. I spent hours, days, months, years with a tea tray on my lap and a pen in my hand, teaching myself to write, to think, and even, slowly, to begin to feel. During the worst years of my crisis, in my early thirties, I sometimes wrote sixteen hours a day, just to find a way to see and experience myself as real.

As long as I felt my hand move across the page, I knew I was still alive. I had no telephone then, so I could not call for help. I sometimes wrote plaintive letters, but usually destroyed them. There was no money for postage anyway. I sat in a large red 1920s-style chair in a corner of the basement of my old church — this place I called home — with only one goal: to try to stay alive as I waded through hell.

Throughout those years I read everything I could get my hands on. I was searching for some hint, some life that resembled mine, that told the truth about the pain I carried. I had a hope I could not express: If I could find anything at all to relate to, the secret that held me in such terror would be unlocked and I would be free at last to begin my life.

I did not feel then that I was living my real life at all. I referred to myself as someone in cold storage, someone trapped under a boulder, someone at the bottom of a pit or in a tunnel from which there was no hope of escape. I felt utterly powerless and unable to change a single thing about my life. I lived in a black hole of depression and despair — a fate against which I thought I could not rebel.

Toward the end of this time, I experienced a new and increasing frustration. It seems to me now that it built as I acquired the words to articulate how I felt. Over my desk and painting table, I hung quotes from women I admired, women who clarified for me what I was trying to do. I have long since forgotten the source of these quotes, but my favourites are still the words of two Afro-American writers, Zora Neale Hurston: "I mean to wrassle me up a future, or die trying," and Alice Walker: "You have to git man off your eyeball, before you can see anything at all."

I still did not have any clear memories of my childhood that I was willing to acknowledge. In fact, I enjoyed the delusion that I had never had a childhood, for that was easier to cope with than recognizing even the smallest part of what childhood had been for me. I eventually began to admit things to myself, like the fact that I hated my father: first for one reason — that he'd beaten me unconscious while my mother was in Europe, visiting her parents; then for two reasons — that he'd refused to feed me in my early teens, or forced me to beg for my dinner, on my knees beside his chair; then more reasons for hating him appeared, slowly. So I wrote them down and wept over my journal pages, thinking each time that this was it, this was why I was a mess, and now that I knew the cause, I'd be fine.

Yet there was always more. And as more incidents surfaced and I wrote about them, I began to feel a little stronger. I still hid in my church basement, not having anything to do with people. But I began to think I might be okay, even as I clung with fierce denial to the notion that I had been the victim of one man's stupidity and rough handling, and nothing more. I still believed, too, that it was my fault. If only I had been more willing, more self-effacing, given him more of what he wanted with less hassle; if only I had been less stubborn, less determined; if only I had been a boy — none of this would have happened. It was my fault. In the words of one of my sisters: I provoked him because I was too stupid not to.

By the spring of 1986 I had a lot of disconnected fragments of memory and a growing determination to write a book about what I was discovering. Reading back through the journals, I find myself writing very generally about "what he did to me," for though the sexual abuse had begun to surface the previous winter, I still found it safer to distance myself from it, as though it had happened to someone I had once known very slightly.

Nothing was clear yet, but the determination to understand what this was really about grew with every page I wrote. I wanted to write about what some men do to their daughters, about male abuse of power, about how religious beliefs are cited as justification for abuse. I wanted to write a book that would make a difference — but I did not yet have the courage to speak. So instead of writing about my childhood, for several years I wrote about writing about my childhood, about the book I would find a way to write one day and what it would look like. I see now that I did all of my planning for the book that became *Don't* during this time.

One day I realized that I had begun to climb the mountain, and as I stopped for a rest I thought to look back to where I had been. The journal I had written during all those years was where I could see this: I had described everything I had experienced, each wretched moment, each tiny step forward and the months and years of just plain being stuck. The journal is an amazing document, unbearably painful reading and one of my greatest personal treasures. Besides being a travelogue of my healing process, it is also where I taught myself to write.

Picking and chipping one's way up the mountain requires a certain amount of skill and an enormous amount of determination. I used words as my tools, but there are others. When I began to feel better about myself, my first thought was that I would now be able to stop writing and finally begin to earn a living. And the first thing I promised myself I would stop writing about was my childhood and my pain. Instead, I realized that the book I knew I would write had finally found me. It was ready. All I had to do was sit at the computer and it was there — flowing from the ends of my fingers as if by magic. Well, almost.

I still fought daily with myself about the need I felt to walk back into hell, face the abusers and write a book about that. No, I said. I don't need to do anything like that. I need to go forward, not backward. I'm going to put all this behind me and get on with my life. Enough of this navel gazing. I said to myself: I like the place I've come to; I don't want to leave the security of it in order to go on. And if I write the book, my life may change more than I want it to, in more ways than I can imagine. I've had enough of this roller-coaster stuff. I want a rest.

I finally realized that the only way things would ever change, the only way I would ever get past the pain I carried, would be to go into it and through it and write from there. No wonder I had avoided this step for so long! The only way I could write this book was to describe the events as though I were experiencing them all over again as a nine-year-old or an eleven-year-old. I had to find, and then write in, the voice of my child self. Nothing else was real enough or carried enough of the pain into the light.

I had a six-week rest, and one morning I got up knowing that, ready or not, I was going to write my book. I was going to do it as fast as I could and hope it would not hurt too much. Fast didn't help; it hurt unbearably. But the important thing is that I kept faith with myself, saw the commitment through, faced each horror-filled day and kept on writing through my tears. I'm immensely proud of that now, and not a little in awe of my determination. For that's what it takes: single-minded determination to walk through the hell of the past, to face all those abusers and demons. And then, with pride in your great courage, to walk tall and strong into sunlight.

As I wrote *Don't*, the pieces of my fragmented self began to approach wholeness; the child who had been beaten, raped and strangled into terror and silence learned to speak as an adult, with compassion and power. The fear-ridden child who had lived with every known phobia learned to face and survive her fears. The self-abusive and unnurtured child learned to take care of herself.

The Inanna myth I used to structure *Don't* is about coming to terms with the darkness, facing my fears, making the descent into the depths of hell and trusting that it is both necessary and, ultimately, healing. My understanding of the myth is that it is about the process of giving up aspects of myself to profound life-renewing change: the quest for my self and my soul. There are, of course, aspects of the myth still closed to me, as there are aspects of my life not yet illuminated. For I have not yet walked the paths or lived the days in which that understanding will come.

It took, in all, thirteen years from the time I began to work on feeling better about myself, before I was ready to begin writing *Don't*. And once I had begun, I wrote as though all the demons in hell were just over my shoulder. I wrote, it seemed, at the speed of light, with a rage and passion I can only look back on in wonder. In less than a month the manuscript was written. Get it over with, I had said, then put it away and you will never have to think about it again.

Well, it didn't quite turn out like that. Fate intervened and brought me, trembling and terrified, to Vancouver in August 1987, to West Word, the school for women writers, and a workshop given by Nicole Brossard. For the first time in my life, my voice was respectfully heard, although, when I read from the manuscript, I read in a barely audible whisper. I received two offers to publish, accepted one before I left Vancouver, and went home in a state of shock.

A month later the copy-edited manuscript was sent back to me from the publisher's office in Charlottetown. Over a ten-day period I argued back and forth with myself about taking it out into the middle of the yard and burning it. I knew in my gut that if I went through with this, if the manuscript was published, my life would change, and I thought I knew, from experience, that it would not change for the better.

Don't was published in Canada in the spring of 1988. The publisher felt there should be no advance publicity. We both feared for my safety, and she wondered, as well, if I would be able to stand up to the pressure and threats that were sure to come my way if it was known by the perpetrators (who lived a mere thirty kilometres away from me) that I planned to make the story of my childhood public.

I look back on the woman who went east to Toronto and Montreal, to launch the book in May 1988, and she seems almost a stranger to me. For she was terrified of travel, terrified of meeting people and absolutely out of her mind with worry about being required to talk about the book and her life.

All those years during which I sat alone, writing and dreaming of a life of strength, of a sure and passionate voice, I didn't really think I could achieve it, didn't think I had the stamina or the courage. Sure I'd been preparing for something, sure I'd laid the groundwork for probably twenty years, but I didn't really think, when all was said and done, that I could find my way through the first week of talking about that book.

T w o

Confronting
the World

How can I begin to describe the reaction to *Don't?* The
phone started to ring, for I had a phone then, and people called from
across the country (when they could get my unlisted phone number), to ask for interviews and with invitations to come to their
communities to speak. Suddenly I was "Ms. Danica" and getting
requests for interviews. No one was more surprised than I was. Does
that describe it? Well, yes and no.

I have been reading the newspaper articles written about me
between 1989 and 1991, and have come away from them wondering
why I have such an unrelieved feeling of disappointment. What is
there to feel disappointed about? Perhaps I am simply frustrated,
seeing how much has been tried and how little has been accom-
plished for children at risk in the intervening years. Perhaps it isn't
disappointment but just a recognition of my reluctance to approach
this material and write about it. For many years it was impossible to

find books by other travellers who had shared my journey. I realize now that not only had I been involved in intense denial about my childhood experience, but society was in denial that these things happened to any child, ever.

Societal denial is often subtle and takes many forms. Soon after *Don't* was published, a *Toronto Star* review of several books about child sexual abuse lauded Sylvia Fraser's *My Father's House* because it had a "polished literary quality ... The threads and themes wind through it with fascinating complexity, like coloured ribbons around a maypole. There was no such patina or literary gloss around *Don't*." Charlotte Vale Allen's *Daddy's Girl* had a "disturbing commercial readability"; *Don't* was an "unyielding scream." At one point, the reviewer, Arlene Perly Rae, wondered why I would write the book at all, and implied that I was still such a mess that I couldn't even cope with interviews. She stated that I had demanded to be interviewed in a church (because nothing else was safe or feasible for me?), missing entirely the fact that the church I was interviewed in was my home. My book was too "infuriating and outrageous to absorb"! It seemed that Fraser's book got Rae's vote because it was a novel and gave the reader those coloured ribbons to hang onto.

While Rae understood what I tried to do with my book, she dismissed it because what I had to say discomfited her. Rae's parting shot was that we who write about child abuse are merely "attempting to get back at [the perpetrator] ... By making him the victim, we find the accused guilty ... duly condemned. Catharsis complete." In this dismissive scenario, unless you are a novelist, you are either too commercial or too loud to be taken seriously. The implication was also that writing the book served a personal purpose and that the issue of child abuse did not have wider significance.

It seemed to me that many of the newspaper interviewers who called me about *Don't* had not taken the time to read the book, for why else would I be asked to describe its contents over and over? An interview, I was to discover, gets an author more publicity than a review because it appears in the first three pages of the newspaper, instead of on the book-review page on the weekend. This was good for the book, but I found the questions gruelling and sometimes appalling.

Why did I have to repeat the events of my childhood, like a litany, over and over and over again? I could never do this without feeling ill, disgusted, horrified. This is what happened? To me? God, how terrible. You want more details? Why, will you print them? I doubt it. Oh, you need more background information. Yes, yes, of course, I see. And the journalists would apologize, knowing, they said, how difficult this must be, but not knowing, really, or they would have found a different way to do this. This was journalistic voyeurism, not news.

It wasn't always like this. Some journalists did take the time to read the book and asked meaningful questions about family reaction; how the promotion tour felt; what my life was like all these years later; what had happened to the offenders; and what my hopes were for the future, for myself and for others with this sort of history. Many of the resulting articles were well done, whatever the words above them said to make me flinch. What is a reader to make of headlines of this ilk: "Book becomes salvation for victim of sexual abuse" and "Life sank into a haze of drugs, promiscuity for 15 year span" and "Father set up her gang rape, writer tells all"? This sensationalizing approach undercut the message I wanted to impart to readers and made the story easy to dismiss. My intent was to inform readers that child abuse is prevalent, and that the suffering of abused children is great and has lifelong implications. I wished to encourage readers to care enough to work together to take whatever steps are necessary to stop the abuse of children.

I learned from these headlines that an issue is coloured by the media's presentation of it. A person is presented in one way if belief in what she says is implied, and another way if what she says is not accepted or is not deemed to be significant. I saw this distinction most clearly in newspaper headlines, but also in introductions on radio and television programs and in the tone of some interviews. The media give readers, listeners or viewers signals as to how to interpret the information or images that are put before them.

It is a function of the medium of print that, at least sometimes, newspaper reporters have time to ask thoughtful questions. I found radio, with the exception of the CBC, more like a fast-food restaurant: I sat in front of the microphone in a studio the size of a broom closet, said my piece and got out. Television was pretty much the same, only with lights and cameras. Nothing can really prepare you for that moment on television when the studio lights are on, the lapel microphone is live and the camera's icy eye is focused on your face. The studio director counts backwards from five. When his hand drops, the command is that you speak, and from somewhere you do find the words, saying for the ten-thousandth time: These things must not be done to children; men must stop abusing kids and women; and yes, these things were done to me.

One of the first problems I encountered with radio and television interviews was getting interviewers to believe my story. Apparently I did not look enough like a victim to be credible. Victims are not, it seems, articulate, clean and tidy; do not travel without a keeper or counsellor; cannot, by their very nature, function in the real world, get to appointments on time, answer questions without collapsing or have an agenda beyond the personal. Victims are in institutions, perhaps; certainly not covering the half-dozen appointments scheduled for that day.

To be credible, it seems I should have looked more like a victim of child abuse. I presume this means I should have been pale, badly dressed, fragile, half carried to interviews, with a therapist on either side of me; with matted hair or in blood-stained clothing, perhaps, like the victim of a car accident or a bomb blast — above all, with visible scars. Dressed as I was, in business attire, with eyes that were not cast down and a clear agenda, how could I be a victim of anything? And even if I once was a victim, it obviously had done me no significant harm. The other side of the story is that if I had looked more like the prevailing notion of a victim, I would have had even less credibility because I would have been dismissed as crazed and unbelievable.

When I was interviewed by reporters sceptical of my story, I was often introduced with a series of greetings that seemed designed to discredit both me and the book. "If what's in this book had really happened to you, you wouldn't be here. You wouldn't have survived." Oh, wouldn't I? "You don't look like a victim, so why would I believe you?" What do victims look like? "If this happened to you, your father must be in jail, right?" Wrong. Other dismissals I encountered included: You are not a Christian; You are a feminist; You hate all men; You refuse to name your father from every public platform; Your sisters and mother don't support your story; You're not affiliated with anyone or anything. Sometimes these statements were made on the air, sometimes just before I had to speak on an open-line show, in an attempt to rattle me or put me on the defensive. At first it certainly was possible to put me on the defensive, but with experience I learned to see where the interview was going and would try to regain my equilibrium so as to be able to say what I needed to.

These dismissals reflect the societal disbelief that has long kept women and children from speaking about their experiences of assault and rape. There were many interviewers who seemed only too ready to believe that male abusers such as my father are the victims of crazy, malicious women who have faulty memories. And I saw this disbelief as a "damned if you do and damned if you don't" situation, for it would be all too convenient for the perpetrators if none of us did speak of what we endured.

In these interviews, the same set of myths were held up as truth: that if I had, in fact, endured what I said I had, I'd be in an institution, living on the street or dead; that fathers who rape their daughters are cretinous monsters who can be easily recognized as such. All too often, when a "respectable" man is accused of child sexual abuse, the community comes to his defence because he's so nice, dresses well and doesn't look like an abuser, while those accused who have the misfortune to fit the popular image of an abuser are written off as surely guilty. If the accused is a teacher, a doctor, a judge — if he appears to be well off or simply attends church regularly — it is believed that he is too upright and educated a citizen to participate in what is still seen as something only the very poorest and least well educated would do, and then only as an adjunct to alcoholism and bad moral fibre.

I was taken aback to discover that, even when interviewers did find my story credible, most focused on what my father and his buddies did. Instead of asking me personal questions about how one can rebuild a life after such abuse, or general questions about the prevalence of child abuse in Canada and what I felt should be done about it, the interviewers wanted to know the details about my particular case, the more lurid and graphic the better — anything, it seemed, to avoid getting to the politics of the issue, to naming who did what to whom and why.

As with the newspaper interviews, what I found most difficult was to be asked, as though somehow it were easy to report all these years later, just what had been done to me when I was four or nine. Why did they have to ask me for the details? So that I could relive in front of the interviewers all that horror and they could watch it connect with my body, discover if it was true, perhaps? Wait to see if I would implode with the telling? Hadn't they read the book? And, of course, they often hadn't. After talking to me they'd talk to somebody about gardening or politics, so it was necessary, once again, for me to summarize the contents of the book, something I could never do without feeling ill. I'd come away from a four-minute television or radio interview emotionally drained, and have to pull myself together in the ten-minute drive across town to the next appointment.

Then there were the interviewers who believed what I had to say but who obviously felt that I carried some of the blame for allowing myself to be victimized. They appeared to think that I must have somehow invited my father's attentions. He was portrayed as a victim of allegations from an angry child and the woman she became. If anyone was actually to be held accountable for child abuse in this scenario, it most certainly was not going to be the perpetrator.

Finally, there were a disturbing number of interviewers who seemed to understand only too well the abuse that I was describing. Or at least, that is what I assumed from observing the reactions of a number of interviewers who seemed threatened by me and responded by being overly aggressive, by being embarrassed or by trying to keep as far away from me as possible.

One man grabbed at me under the table on the set of a television open-line show; I had to respond to a heart-rending phone call from a mother who suspected that her three-year-old child was being abused, while fending off the guy's hands. A radio talkshow host grinned and leered through the hour, seeming to experience an almost pornographic enjoyment of the pain and humiliation the callers spoke of. Another man asked obnoxious questions while trying to lean out of camera range, tilting his chair so far back that I thought for sure he would crash to the floor. I even met a few men who reacted to me with outright fear, physically backing away as I was introduced. On two occasions, when introductions were being effected, men grabbed their private parts in what seemed to be a protective manoeuvre.

When I went to a radio or television station I was usually accompanied by a woman from one of the organizations sponsoring my reading or speech. When I was asked questions about services in the community, the local woman would be able to supply the correct information. When such questions were not anticipated, I would often go to the appointment alone. I was generally briefed by the members of the host committee about what to expect from interviewers, and often a pre-interview with someone from the committee would be set up to familiarize me with the groundwork for the interview.

I approached the interview that autumn day with no reservations. I had been assured that it would be straightforward. When I walked into the studio and was introduced to the interviewer, he shook hands with me and we settled into the chairs on the set for the program. The lights were turned up, the microphone volumes were checked, the television cameras were focused on my face and his, and suddenly the interviewer went on the attack.

After a brief introduction, he opened the interview with the pronouncement: "You hate all men." He progressed from there to ever-more-inflammatory statements, culminating in the accusation that I was acting on a personal vendetta. Never once did the interviewer appear willing to consider that children are sexually abused by their fathers or by other men in the child's immediate family.

I was presented with a conundrum. How was I to deal with such hostility? My reaction was to become even more polite than usual, firmly denying the words and ideas the interviewer belligerently stated were mine, but that had no relationship to anything I had ever said or thought. This merely enraged him further, and his baiting and cutting remarks became even more outrageous. I was tempted several times to react, but you can't win if you argue with this sort of thing, so I did my best to ignore his behaviour and to say what I needed to say to those who might be watching, and fervently hoped the ordeal would soon be over. This memorable event took place in Kingston, Ontario, and in response, a viewer wrote a scathing letter to the *Kingston Whig-Standard* demanding that the man who had conducted this farce of an interview be fired and no longer allowed to infect the screen.

On the way out of the studio, I had to fight the man for my reading copy of the book. He refused to return it, even when I asked him three times politely to hand it over. I had to grab for it, taking it out of his hands. This was my annotated copy; I wasn't about to leave it behind. Once I was out of the television station after this interview, I experienced a sudden and overpowering exhaustion, which made me realize just how much tension had built in me.

In one year I toured from Willowbunch, Saskatchewan, to Dublin, Ireland — via Regina, Winnipeg, Vancouver, Toronto, Montreal, Amsterdam, Munich and dozens of places in between — speaking to thousands of people about the mistreatment and assault endured by children. I was ill prepared for such a public life, for a constant, daily baring of my body and soul's deepest pain, for living in a spotlight perpetually turned on my childhood suffering, and too rarely on the person I had become despite or because of it or on the general issue of child abuse that I felt needed to be addressed.

A friend of mine in Toronto, Barry Lipton, sent a letter and a copy of *Don't* to Peter Gzowski, host of the CBC Radio program *Morningside*, at a time when Peter was planning a trip west that would include a speaking engagement in Moose Jaw. Phone calls from *Morningside*: Would I be willing to do an interview? What would make it possible? After some discussion and assurances, I agreed, stunned. Peter Gzowski, a legend, is coming here, to my house? I was assured by *Morningside* staff that he was deeply moved by my story and would be sensitive in his handling of the interview.

Morningside is broadcast across Canada from 9:00 A.M. to noon each weekday. The program has a large following, and is one of the best ways to bring a topic or a book to the attention of the Canadian public. I once heard an interview in which Peter Gzowski asked a panel of writers the three best ways to sell books in Canada, and the reply was "*Morningside, Morningside, Morningside!*" Added to this is Peter's famous style of interviewing, and his sensitivity. In my opinion and experience, this was by far the most profound media interview I had for *Don't*.

The first thing I think about when somebody is coming to my house is what food I can offer. This almost always presents a crisis. What food can I *afford* to offer? So I cleaned house and organized lunch, trying not to think about whether people would want to eat anything here once they saw how I lived. I am always apologetic about my house, how primitive it is, how like a construction site, how lacking in so many important ways — the lack of plumbing being a particular concern. Focused on these things, I tried not to worry myself into a state.

Four people showed up for the interview: Peter, a technician from Regina and two producers from Toronto. We chatted on the front steps, then the crew came in while Peter stayed outside to finish a cigarette. I answered questions from the crew about how long I had lived in this old church, and about life in a village of a hundred people.

The interview with Peter Gzowski took two hours. I was so tense, so worried I'd make a fool of myself, so worried about the questions I'd have to answer, so terrified that I'd unravel completely, that I had a fierce headache. We seated ourselves at opposite ends of the sofa, the technician in a chair across from us, and the rest of the crew went to sit outdoors.

Peter was sensitive in his approach to the questions, and I think his compassion is clear in the broadcast interview. I found it an amazing experience to be treated with such gentleness and care, and it is still there in Peter's voice whenever he speaks about me. He didn't skirt the issues in any way, for he is a persistent interviewer, but neither did he pressure me, assuring me that I could take my time and respond in whatever way I felt was comfortable and appropriate. And when he asked me to speak about something I felt I could not bear to talk about, I was able to say, "I can't go there," and he was willing either to let it go or to approach it differently.

After the interview I went for a walk, replaying the scene, the interview, over and over in my mind and wondering what would come of it once it got to Toronto and was prepared for radio broadcast. This was the most amazing experience in a time of incredible experiences. The broadcast was to prove just how amazing it all was.

The day of the broadcast, I sat in my chair in the upstairs studio of my old church. If disaster had struck the building that morning, I could not have moved if I'd wanted to. The power of the interview horrified me and made me weep for the child who had endured so much pain. I sat motionless, pinned in that chair for three hours before I could get up, so overwhelmed was I by what I had heard, and by my fear of what this would mean.

The broadcast made me even more nervous and afraid than I had been until then: worried that my father and his cronies would hear of it and take revenge. What would my siblings do? Or my mother? What would this oh-so-public exposure of the story mean to my life? These were questions I had also asked around the time of the book's publication, of course, but my thought now was that people can ignore a book — I was pretty sure my family had done just that — but I didn't think it would be possible for anyone to ignore this interview.

As it turned out, there was little immediate local response, although I understand the switchboard at CBC Toronto lit up and stayed that way for hours as people in various time zones called to talk about the interview.

During the next two years I heard numerous stories about people's reactions: the woman who was so intent on listening that, when somebody ran into her car in a parking lot, she told the culprit to go away because she was busy; people who were driving when they heard the interview and had to stop their cars because they couldn't see where they were going through their tears; women who said they wanted to turn the radio off but found they could not; and people who have that morning forever imprinted in their memories, as they told me, "like the day J.F.K. was shot."

I felt more exposed and vulnerable than ever before, and also more profoundly alone. It is terrifying to go public in this way — once people knew who I was, they would stop on the street and stare at me as though I was some sort of freak and very, very dangerous.

I heard from friends that some people in Moose Jaw interpreted what I had to say as: She says she "slept with" her father, not she was "raped as a child," thereby making the child, and not the adult perpetrator, responsible for the abuse. The difference in language is not slight or insignificant: saying the child slept with her father essentially means that the speaker denies there is a problem. Acknowledging that the child was raped implies belief in the child, and in the fact that a crime has been committed against her for which the perpetrator should bear sole responsibility.

To those people who chose to see the issue as "she slept with her father," I had simply proven my worthlessness as a poor immigrant kid from the wrong side of town. Others, missing the point entirely, referred to me as the writer of "that sex book," implying that I had written something lurid and pornographic. By seeing the book in this light, these people were able to avoid dealing with that most uncomfortable and dangerous of topics: the sexual assault of children. There were still others who dismissed me as vicious and crazy, knowing, as they said, my "nice guy" father. With their refusal to believe what I had written, they did not have to revisit assumptions they held about who my father really was.

Yet others — many, many others — shuddered at the thought that their sisters, daughters, nieces and granddaughters had been in that man's photography studio as putative "models." It seemed to be absolutely clear to people in Moose Jaw who the book was about, even though my name is not the same as my father's and I had not lived in Moose Jaw for more than twenty years.

It is, contrary to some things I have heard, appalling to be celebrated as a victim. It is a millstone that grows heavier as you drag it around with you. I guess there was an assumption in some of the media interviews that I had written the book because I was desperate to talk about the abuse — as though public exposure on radio and television was my preferred therapeutic context, a peculiar conceit of too many open-line shows. When I made the decision to hand over the manuscript for publication, I had almost no knowledge of what that would mean. I believed the abusers should be exposed and their crimes against children shown clearly. But it wasn't my father and his cronies who were placed in the spotlight, having to explain and justify their actions — it was me.

My message for other victims of child abuse was that it is important to talk to someone you trust; that unresolved child-abuse trauma is a very dangerous thing to leave buried; that the pain and terror can be survived and can be healed. Yet, in order to deliver this message, I had to speak constantly about my own past, in excruciating detail, and I had to read from the book I had written to put my past firmly behind me.

I don't mean to disparage the many thoughtful and sensitive professional journalists I met who did their best to make me comfortable during interviews, and who gave me the opportunity to say what I felt was important to say. It is the process I want to critique. At the beginning I thought, all too briefly, that this attention from the media was the same as attention from society as a whole. I imagined that the attention I and several other writers in the 1980s received as we worked to highlight the issue of child abuse implied a societal and political will to do something about it. But all too soon today's issue becomes yesterday's news. Worse, there's a perception that, once an issue has spent several months in the spotlight, it has been dealt with, and the implication seems to be that it is thereby resolved.

As any survivor of child sexual abuse can attest, nothing about this issue is simple, and no aspect of it allows for quick and easy resolution. Certainly six months or so of media attention is not the same as an extensive societal commitment to doing what needs to be done to stop violence against children. Yet, as I discovered early on in my book promotion-tour with *Don't*, it is this complexity that stands in the way of effective programs to address the needs of abused children, adult survivors of abuse and perpetrators. In order to deal with these needs, we as a society must take the time to examine all our beliefs and practices affecting children. Rather than embark upon this daunting task, we all too quickly sweep these important issues back under the carpet — the ultimate excuse being that it is really much too costly to address them.

Three

Becoming a Public Person

  I'm thinking about the process of acquiring a public persona. How did I get from being such a quivering lump to feeling comfortable in public, even with the miserable topic I talked about daily? I am retracing my steps, looking for the crumbs on the forest floor that will lead me back to the person I was at the beginning of the journey. Perhaps she cannot be recovered, but I try because I need to understand. When I began, I was so fragile. There were things that would have made life easier for me then; at the very least, I should have had a friend to travel with, or some previous experience of travel.

  I didn't write *Don't* with any conscious notion that I wanted it to be published. My hope was to ease the pain in my soul. I thought that if I could tell the truth about my experience of childhood, I would accomplish that much. More than this I didn't consider. No writer really writes only for herself, however. She may begin by writing what is essential for her to write for herself alone, but gradually she will discover that she wants to find a reader. I had great difficulty acknowledging a desire to be heard and read. Anyone whose self-esteem was low as mine was at that time is more comfortable apologizing for her existence than promoting a book.

In this state of mind I arrived in Montreal for the International Feminist Book Fair in June 1988, a couple of months after the book was released in Canada. There I met writers I had long admired, and my reaction was either incoherence or speechlessness. I was afraid they would find out I wasn't a real writer, for I didn't think I was one. I was utterly out of my depth, and overwhelmed. Years spent isolated and alone ill equipped me for speaking to people. Here I was given warm wishes and congratulations by women I held in awe, and all I could think of was how to apologize for the book, my life, everything. I wasn't happy or exhilarated by the attention — I was terrified.

Gynergy books had a booth at the fair. I sat there with the then-publisher, who introduced me to writers she knew. By far the best part of the experience was to be around so many books. I would happily have spent thousands of dollars, had I had the money. I may have been shy and nervous about meeting the authors, but I was delighted to be in the presence of their work.

The rest of the experience was another matter. I didn't feel comfortable in the city, among so many people. I was afraid of my own shadow, afraid to walk alone from the hall where the fair was held to the dorm. I was anxious about my threadbare, dowdy clothing, worried I didn't look "right," whatever that was. I felt I had been plucked out of my equivalent of an isolated cabin in the woods, where I had lived without television, without newspapers, and plunked down in the middle of Montreal with no more than a "See yah. Have a good time." Nobody who hasn't been through this can easily understand how hard it was. I was intimidated by everyone. I didn't know how to cope, but I didn't want anyone to know because I was ashamed of being so frightened of ordinary things.

I wouldn't go into a restaurant by myself, wouldn't get on a bus or into a taxi by myself. If I couldn't find anyone to go out with, I'd stay in my room. I had no basis for coping in Montreal or most other cities. In Toronto there was my friend Barry Lipton, who would take me to what I wanted to see, and I wasn't afraid he'd sneer at me for being so childishly afraid. He understood my fear better than anyone. He also gave me the best analysis of the problem: "You have no city skills," he said. "That's nothing to be ashamed of."

I still don't have city skills. I still get into a nervous state when I have to navigate in any city by myself, so I try to avoid it. I do now enjoy being in a city as long as I'm with someone who doesn't mind me tagging along. But at the end of a day of wandering around, I still find myself panic-stricken and tense. It's not hard to understand why: I live in a tiny village and never see anyone; if the phone rings twice a week, I think it's been busy. To go from this lifestyle to a bustling city is difficult, but no longer absolutely terrifying.

On the whole, this feminist book fair experience remains a blur. It was there that my publisher began negotiations for foreign-rights sales. Within the next eighteen months, there were eight editions of *Don't* in print: English-language editions published by The Women's Press in the United Kingdom, Attic Press in Ireland and Cleis Press in the United States; a German translation published by Frauenoffensive in Munich; a Dutch translation published by An Dekker in Amsterdam; and a French translation published by Les éditions du remue-ménage in Montreal; and a mass-market edition published by McClelland & Stewart in Canada.

I got back to my prairie church near the end of June, so tense and exhausted that I slept most of the next ten days. At the end of that time, I was physically rested but not at all settled in my mind. I needed to talk to somebody, but I was afraid to so much as own that I had written a book, never mind talk about what was now happening to it outside Saskatchewan. And if I couldn't bring myself to talk to anyone, then I wanted something physically challenging to do that would take my mind off what was happening.

I decided, with no carpentry skills whatsoever, to build myself a bed. For years my studio had been cluttered with several huge pieces of lumber: 2x10s and 2x12s I kept tripping over no matter where I stacked them. I had always intended to move them, but one of them was over five metres long and was too heavy even to drag anywhere else. I drew up a plan and made a list of the pieces of lumber I needed. I positioned the boards across three chairs and cut them with a handsaw. Once they were cut, I took the boards out to the yard, where I had a double cast-iron laundry sink I used as a workbench. There I sanded the individual pieces to reveal the lovely warm honey colour of the fir, and as I did that I meditated on what I was going to do.

It took me three weeks to cut, sand and apply several coats of Varathane to the boards and to assemble the bed. By the time it was finished I had a plan. What was the point, I asked myself, of hiding or running away? The book was attracting positive notice. Why didn't I just see where it would go, and enjoy the attention? And how would I do that? I had much to learn to make the most of the opportunities the book gave me. I had to learn how to respond to the public without collapsing completely, either psychologically or physically. I had to learn what I was willing to do or talk about that would leave me on my feet and functioning at the end of the day and the week. I had to train myself in public speaking and presentation, and learn how to cope with the hundreds of disclosures I knew I would hear.

There is no workshop I know of where a writer can go to learn to respond to the public: to learn how to prepare for everything from radio and television appearances and interviews to book-signing sessions, to standing at podiums in large auditoriums. There are no deportment, dressing and make-up workshops for the freshly launched author who has spent most of her life in clothes from thrift stores and who doesn't own any make-up. Still less is there advice on how to talk to people and respond appropriately to so much pain. And even if there had been such help, there was suddenly no time.

Peter Gzowski's interview, broadcast in November 1988, catapulted the book into national public awareness. I began to receive letters from readers, as well as from people who had heard the interview on *Morningside*: letters that thanked me for the book, lauded my courage and often contained pain-filled descriptions of the writer's childhood experiences. Although I was glad that the book and the interview were well thought of, reading those letters sent me into an intensely worried state. I didn't know what it was appropriate to do with the excruciatingly painful disclosures being shared with me.

It was not a solution for me to write a generic response and fire it off to every person who wrote to me, yet what could I say to the writer that would offer anything in the way of comfort for her pain or encouragement for her healing? I didn't have enough faith in myself to believe that anything I said in a letter might be useful, and I was fearful of unwittingly causing additional pain. I would agonize to such an extent over each letter that I often couldn't reply, and I regret that now. I think a simple and straightforward acknowledgement was what many of the women were looking for. Somehow, when I talked to a woman in person, I found it easier to respond to her pain with compassion, for I did trust my skill at reading faces. At first overwhelmed by the public reaction *Don't* had unleashed, I gradually came to feel I could meet and respond to women who had stories like mine.

I began to relax into the job of being an author. As painful and difficult as it often was at the beginning, it was in many ways a role I enjoyed. I found, much to my surprise, that I loved meeting people, loved the role of author on tour and all that it implied in terms of dining in restaurants, travel and public recognition. I felt this was a holiday of sorts, because I was away from my desk and my worries about the current writing project and whether or not I'd eat this week. I got into a routine and felt for a while that this was my life. It was much more fun, even with talking about child abuse incessantly, than sitting still to sort out the problems with my childhood that remained. Everything else in my life was on hold. I allowed myself no worries other than making it on time to my next appointment, or to the airport for the flight to the next city.

The first few times I stood before an audience to read from the book, I found it arduous and painful. My knees quaked, and my voice wouldn't cooperate and would run out of air or falter when I most needed it. I locked my knees to keep myself upright, but this felt much too tense. I found that if I sat to read I was more comfortable and could do a better job. Eventually, with experience, I grew more at ease with being at a podium or on stage.

Audiences always carefully scrutinize the people they are there to see. The questions I was asked astonished me at first. Why would anybody want to know whether I had a relationship with a man? Why would anybody care what my religious beliefs were or were not? Often I'd answer questions for forty-five minutes or longer after a lengthy reading from the book. These questions, I later learned, were almost always to do with information the individual needed for her own life. Face to face, the woman would tell me the story behind the question she had asked in the public forum.

One woman was concerned that she would not be able to sustain her relationship with her boyfriend if he found out about the abuse. Another felt she would be ostracized by her church group if she told, and feared her faith would not withstand such a rift. Many women feared that the truth about their childhoods would permanently sever their relationships with family members. If I said I was involved with a man, maybe the questioner could one day feel comfortable in such a relationship. If I said I was a Christian believer, maybe the questioner could find a way to reconnect with her own lost faith. But I had to tell the truth. No, I wasn't yet comfortable around men. No, I wasn't a Christian. And, most difficult of all, each family — indeed, each family member — responds differently to child-abuse disclosures. But, I told my audiences, my personal situation mattered less than what the women asking the questions felt comfortable with. Just because something was not possible for me did not mean it would be impossible for someone else.

I became aware that some people believed that, although women like me could cope with a miserable past, it was beyond their own powers and strengths. For example, a woman would preface a question with the statement that she was sure she would never find the courage to face the abuse she had endured or to tell her mother about it. So I would say, "Well, it took great courage for you to come here tonight. If you could do that, you have plenty of courage for the work ahead on the path to feeling better about yourself, whatever that work is for you."

Interaction with audience members at my readings was often intensely personal, with many people telling me what they had never before told anyone. Some days it seemed that each story was more terrible than the last. And the women, for it was most often women, said they had to tell me because they were certain I would understand; and that nobody until then had ever understood their sorrow and pain or accepted it as true. Many nights I heard fifty or more stories, holding the hand of each woman as we talked for a couple of minutes after I signed a book for her.

The atmosphere at these public events was often intensely charged, and never more so than during the reading I did for the Moose Jaw Public Library. This was my home town and the abusers still lived here. I assumed this would be a vicious and hostile audience. I had requested a police presence in the audience and I sat with a librarian on either side of me to make me feel safer. This was the only venue in which I feared for my personal safety. The auditorium booked for the reading could hold 150 people, and forty minutes before I was to appear, a huge crowd had arrived to hear me. The room could accommodate no more people, and still they came, standing in the adjacent park until the outside crowd was even larger than the one seated inside. A couple of quick-thinking local writers got in touch with the custodian of a much larger hall in the church across the street and quickly moved the crowd and sound system to the new location. An estimated 350 to 400 people heard me speak that night and, although it was very tense, there proved to be no need for the police.

Speaking out about the book was incredibly exhausting work, but I felt it was helping to make a difference, for so many women told me how the book had changed their lives and how much it meant to them to have a chance to see me in person. I saw it as an extension of my original project, which had been to ease my own pain; if these public appearances helped ease the pain of others, how could I refuse to do them?

I received many requests to attend promotional events for the book, and it became apparent that, if I wanted to, I could travel regularly. Carolyn Guertin, a friend who is a skilled publicist, stepped in to organize tours and speaking engagements I could not have undertaken without her help. She handled the details, called people, made contact with potential sponsors, set up media appointments and interviews and worked out exquisitely detailed schedules. If I spent months on the road, Carolyn spent months on the phone organizing it all. My only regret is that she was not paid more for the work she did. My earnings in one city paid to keep me going until the money came in from the next engagement. Life on the road is not cheap, and I had my home in Saskatchewan to maintain while I was away.

I began the longest of my three tours in January 1990, on my birthday, speaking to inmates in Pinegrove, the prison for women in Prince Albert, Saskatchewan. The first thing I saw when I walked into the institution was a group of women with their arms extended through the bars of the main gate, palms upward, waiting for the warder to give them their medications. My reading was held in the auditorium, only a few steps inside the gate. It was one of the most difficult presentations I made, for the room I spoke in was filled with the pain and tension of women who lived behind bars. I couldn't help but think, there but for the grace of the angels go I. I thought about the horror of incarceration, and what it is like to have no choices about anything, a situation entirely too close to the reality of my childhood. I found it devastating to spend even an hour in this environment, and I cried for hours on the trip back to Regina.

From Saskatchewan I flew west to Edmonton, Calgary, Lethbridge, Vancouver, Salmon Arm, Victoria, Ganges, and Saltspring Island. The engagements were all roughly the same. I would be given a finalized appointment schedule for my visit when I was met at the airport. Next I'd be driven to the hotel to check in, or to a billet home to drop off my luggage. If there was time, there would be a quick tour of the community, including the sponsoring agency's office. In Edmonton, it was Catholic Family Services; in many other places, it was a coalition of community groups formed specifically to raise public awareness about violence against women and children. Then the person whose task it was to take me around to all the appointments in the next few days would find a suitable restaurant, and over coffee or lunch would give me an overview of the situation in the community regarding the issue of child sexual abuse.

In most communities I visited there were basic services available for the protection of children, and even more services for adult survivors of child abuse. Counselling and support services, however, often had lengthy waiting lists. Every community wanted to do more, and it was felt that increasing public awareness was a logical first step.

Most often the person who took me around to my appointments was a woman who did this along with all the myriad responsibilities of her regular job and family life. Many times I wished I could spend more time in a place just so there would be more time to visit with the women I met. In every community I was treated with amazing care and concern for my well-being and comfort. In Edmonton, when I mentioned in some context I can't even remember — maybe during an interview — that I was allergic to wheat and found it difficult to find appropriate food while travelling, the owner of a bakery sent me a dozen loaves of rice bread, with best wishes.

In the evening there would be a dinner with the committee who had organized the event that had brought me to the community. This was where I met the women and men who worked to make their communities better and safer places for children and people at risk, through women's and church groups and volunteer organizations. Occasionally these dinners were formal, but more often they were wonderfully warm, and with laughter and wit celebrated the committee's success in organizing a coalition.

I would learn about the services the community offered (women's shelters, counselling, programs for abused kids and adults) and what the committee hoped my visit would do in terms of raising awareness of the prevalence of child abuse. I would be briefed about the interviews and what to expect from the interviewers, when that was known. Wherever possible, I liked to do the interviews on one day and the speaking engagement on another — to make sure I had a voice and not merely a croaking sound for my readings, and also to keep the pace from becoming impossibly hectic, for after two and a half days or so I would be off to do the same thing in the next community, and then the one after that. Pacing was an early and important consideration for me.

The city of Victoria, on Vancouver Island, was my winter destination, and by late January I had arrived. I spent a week visiting with my nineteen-year-old son, Greg. We went to his favourite cappuccino and dessert places, tried all sorts of different restaurants, spent ages in bookshops, saw the sights, and talked and talked. It was the first visit we had had in two years, and the first visit on his turf rather than mine. I had not seen Greg since he had read *Don't*, and we had a lot of catching up to do. It was during this visit that we began a new phase of our relationship, for he was now an adult, and one who was intensely proud of his mother and what she was doing.

After spending time with Greg, I went to the Gulf Islands to recuperate from my months of touring. The owners of Spindrift, a lovely resort on Saltspring Island, had given me the gift of a two-week stay. A reading had been organized to cover my expenses, and several local women were to keep the little guest cabin I stayed in supplied with firewood. By the time I got there, I was very much in need of rest, and this was the perfect place — stunningly beautiful and quiet (no phone, television or radio), yet only a few minutes from town and cappuccino. I slept, read, walked, and in the evenings I dreamt in front of the fireplace. It was heaven, and I dream of returning for another visit. Without this gift, I doubt that I could have carried on through the next few months. It would be late May before I could again have a relaxing, quiet time.

All too soon the time on Saltspring Island was over and I headed back east, bound for the city, media interviews and speaking engagements. My calendar for the month of March tells me I was in Toronto, Hamilton, London, Sault Ste. Marie, Montreal and Regina. In Sault Ste. Marie I had a severe allergy attack, complicated by a cold and exhaustion, that landed me in a hospital emergency room because I couldn't breathe. I had struggled through an interview, and every few minutes the microphone had had to be shut off as I coughed and coughed. After the interview, which I refused to quit even when it was suggested that I do so, the woman who had been taking me to my various appointments insisted that we go to emergency at the hospital. The doctor told me to stop what I was doing, rest, take it easy. I can't, I said. People are counting on me. I have to be in Montreal tomorrow.

By the end of March I was back in Saskatchewan to do a reading tour of several rural libraries and to speak at a conference in Regina. Then I returned to my boarded-up home to search through boxes for clothes for the next stage of the trip, and back east to Toronto for the flight to Europe.

I arrived at Toronto airport in mid-April, bound for Amsterdam. All my tour-related expenses and travel were covered for this European trip, but I had only a couple of hundred dollars in personal spending money to see me through seven weeks. I called Barry, asked him to keep me company during the five hours between planes. We had coffee, talked about the itinerary. He gave me travel hints and we visited. Then he handed me a thick envelope. He's not the sort who gives cards, so I was surprised. I opened the envelope to find a wad of money. "What's this?" I asked in amazement. "Fifteen hundred dollars, U.S.," he said. "So you can relax and have a good time." I wanted to know where he had got this much money. "Where do you think? A bank, of course. That's what banks are for — to borrow money, eh," he said, laughing at my astonishment as I looked alternately at the money and at him. "This is really wonderful," I said, "but are you sure? It's so much." "Don't worry about it," he said. "Enjoy it."

Arrival in Holland: landing in a dream I had been dreaming for thirty-eight years. I wanted to rush out to see, experience and touch everything at once. Most of all, I wanted to listen to people speaking Dutch, the language of my mother and her mother, the lost language of my early childhood. My Oma (grandmother) was still alive, age ninety-four, in a nursing home in Wageningen. But I was nervous about going to see her, fearing I suppose, several things: yet more rejection from someone related to me, or finding a woman to whom old age had not been kind and whose mind was no longer intact. I had no way of knowing, for though I had sent cards and occasionally received cards in return, no real information could be exchanged; my grandmother did not understand English and I could not write in Dutch. It had been several years since I had heard anything directly from her, and even my mother no longer received regular letters because writing had become too difficult for my grandmother's arthritic hands.

My sense of Holland was a combination of nostalgia for what little I remembered and the magical place my imagination and my yearning for my grandmother's love had made of it. Certainly I ascribed to it culture, art and history such as I had not been able to find in tiny provincial 1950s Moose Jaw. I knew nothing about Holland's contemporary culture, politics or reality — and I no longer spoke Dutch, so I assumed my access to anything would be limited.

Amsterdam in a warm spring sunshine: The trees were greening and every street corner, it seemed, had a flower stall. Every day I walked through the old city streets and along the canals, absorbing the feel, sounds and sights of what I saw as my mother's and my grandmother's city. This was the city they both loved, where my mother had lived until she was twenty-five years old. I hoped my explorations would somehow help me feel closer to my mother; in fact, I learned a great deal about myself.

I visited galleries, a civic museum, a museum of antiquities, numerous antique shops and the Delft shop in the centre of the city, but it was not until I visited the maritime museum that I got a clear sense of who my ancestors really were. When I saw the ships the Dutch had built and the instruments they had designed to sail the open seas, I felt an intense pride and connection — here were people who made the best of a tiny, waterlogged country, and to do so they became expert craftsmen. Craftsmanship has always impressed me, and there is a Dutch sense of craftsmanship and meticulousness that I have most definitely inherited.

I spent most of my three weeks in Holland thinking about my mother. I wondered what it must have been like for her as a young woman during the war in occupied Holland. I grew more and more puzzled about why a young woman with a privileged upper-middle-class background would become so enamoured of a man she had met through a personal ad in a newspaper that she would bolt from her family and marry him. Perhaps it was the climate of the times: the hunger, the fear, the random and not so random brutalities of six years of war.

In Amsterdam I walked through the old city, looking at houses two, three and four hundred years old; wandered through the flower market, along the canals; purchased brined herring with chopped onions from street vendors; sat in the sun, sipping strong coffee, or rested on a bench in the Begijnhof (a group of houses and two chapels surrounding a courtyard, originally founded by a group of women called the Beguines in 1346); toured the royal palace; and spent days in the Rijksmuseum. I began to find my personal connection to my Dutch ancestry, the culture and the language, which nourished a part of me I had long thought was lost in the move to Canada.

If Amsterdam is associated for me with my mother, The Hague, my birthplace, is associated with my father. I know I didn't do it justice, taking a bus tour through it. Perhaps with the opportunity to explore further, I would find it has its fine points, but I found nothing there to engage me the way Amsterdam had from the moment I set foot in it. However, a wonderful moment of serendipity took place in The Hague when I bought a ticket for the bus tour. Over the cash register in the tourist office there was a sign offering tickets for the Van Gogh exhibition. I had stood in line for an hour and a half a few days earlier at the museum ticket kiosk only to be told there were no tickets available during the time I was in Holland. Now I found a ticket for a day I was free to go — what luck!

Since my early twenties, when I first encountered Van Gogh's paintings in a library book, I have had a passion for them. To be able to see the largest exhibition of Van Gogh's works assembled this century was a great delight and a mixed blessing all at once. The ticket entitled the holder to about two hours in the Van Gogh museum. Never having been to an extravaganza of this order, I had no idea what this meant. At the appointed hour, 1,500 tourists swarmed into the museum, standing eight to ten deep in front of each painting. It was impossible to move until or unless the crowd moved. It was also impossible to see anything.

Around me I heard German, American, Italian, French, Spanish and Japanese exclamations about paintings I was too short to see. If I was going to make anything of my two hours in the museum, strategy was required. I looked for the flow pattern in the crowd, to see if there was a way to move in closer to the paintings, but, packed like sardines as we were, I saw nothing until — halfway down a long gallery — the crowd opened briefly to allow someone to pass. Edging my way down to this place took precious minutes, but paid off, and I saw the Van Gogh exhibit in the wake of a wheelchair. To see two hundred paintings in two hours means you have twenty to thirty seconds to glance at each image — not my idea of the best way to view great art. Outside the gallery, enterprising young people had set up spirit stoves with big pots on them and were doing a brisk trade in bowls of potato soup for those interested in the total Van Gogh experience. This made me roar with laughter.

It took me more than a week to find the courage to visit my grandmother, who lived a short distance by train from Amsterdam. I had no luck finding anyone available to go with me to translate for this visit. I wondered who this ancient woman would turn out to be, for surely she was someone quite different from my long-held image of her from nearly forty years earlier. I met a very frail and beautiful old woman whose immediate response to me was one of suspicion. No amount of telling her, with limited Dutch, that I was her granddaughter Elly seemed to make any impression. Perhaps she was deaf? I didn't know and there was no one to ask. I wasn't surprised by her response because she was not expecting my visit, but I was disappointed.

Eventually we did manage to communicate slightly. I found a photograph of her daughter and, pointing to it, said — in what was no doubt an appalling attempt at Dutch — that the woman was my mother. My grandmother became impatient then. She asked what was wrong with me and what had happened to my Dutch. It wasn't exactly my dream of a reunion with her, and I don't think I handled it very well, but I had had a superstitious dread of announcing myself by letter, worried that she would refuse to see me; and I didn't think I could bear that, so I had chosen to simply turn up.

BEYOND DON'T

Surprises can be difficult enough for old folks, never mind when they haven't seen the unexpected visitor for thirty-eight years.

But still she was my Oma, crippled with rheumatism, nearly blind and bed-bound, and I was glad I was able to visit with her, even for such a brief time. The room in which she lived contained old photographs of her children and grandchildren in small frames set on the furniture, while on the otherwise blank wall beside her bed hung an image of the crucified Christ. On the window sill stood a vase with flowers. She was well cared for and her room seemed comfortable, but I wondered how often she was visited by her daughter who lived in France, or by either of her sons who still lived in Holland. I had never met my aunt or two of my three uncles, though the youngest of my mother's brothers did visit once or twice when he lived in Canada for a time. I knew nothing about my mother's siblings, who had not been part of my childhood in any way.

Ten days later I saw my Oma again, and this time I had a translator and the welcome I had so long dreamt of. At one point my grandmother said, "You had a rough time at the start but I see you are doing well now." Again she demanded to know what had happened to my Dutch, and why I no longer spoke it. The translator tried to explain, but no explanation satisfied my Oma; she pretty much said there was no excuse. I told her, through the translator, how much it meant to me to see her and how wonderful it felt to be in Holland after all this time. I presented her with a copy of the Dutch edition of *Don't*, and for me this was a most profound moment. For even though I knew she would never read it, I had finally kept the promise I had made to her in 1952, at the airport, just before I boarded the plane for Canada — the promise to tell her if I was ever again assaulted by my father. The fact that she couldn't now read the book didn't matter; I had closed the circle for myself by writing it and placing a copy in her hands.

The drive from Holland to Hamburg — at 160 kilometres an hour, faster than I'd ever imagined moving in a car — was five hours on the autobahn with my hands clenched in white-knuckled fear as other cars passed at speeds well over 200 kilometres an hour. A man from the Department of External Affairs had offered to drive me to Hamburg, but when we arrived, he was disappointed to be told by the women's centre that the reading was a women-only event. In Germany and Ireland it had been decided to hold women-only events so the women attending would be more comfortable hearing what I had to say. In Canada all events were open to men, though they always made up a very small part of the audience, most often as support for partners who had been abused. During the period I toured with *Don't*, men were rarely willing to speak about abuses they themselves had endured.

A fifth-floor apartment in a Turkish quarter of Hamburg, on loan to me for the weekend: As a result of the terror I had of going out alone in a city I didn't know, I spent my time in the apartment writing, trying to ground myself and prepare for the gruelling week ahead while delighting in the blossoms of the most magnificent cherry tree I had ever seen. I was fascinated by the tree because of its size and splendour, the crown being just outside the apartment window. In the courtyard below, I saw a couple prepare and enjoy a picnic at a battered table under the tree. I also saw bullet holes in the walls around the courtyard. The assurances that they were from the last war didn't do a bit to make me feel safe, and it was the beautiful cherry tree alone that kept me from bolting to an airport and the first plane for Canada I could find.

Muenster: I arrived late in the afternoon in a city that, on the surface, was beautiful. The woman who met me at the train station asked me if I would like to take a walk and see the sights. Most of the centre of the city had been destroyed in the last war and some of it has been rebuilt. In the centre is St. Lamberts, a church like no other. Hanging from the spire of the clock tower was what I took to be scaffolding, for safety reasons perhaps. No, the young woman with me said, not scaffolding — cages. Oh, I thought, that's what they call scaffolding here. No, she said again, softly — for heretics. The guidebook I later consulted said that the corpses of the Anabaptist leaders were hung in the three cages after the bishop's troops quelled their rebellion in 1535 — a chilling reminder of what horrors people are capable of in any age.

The women I met in Germany were familiar with English, American and Canadian feminist authors, and though time was short, I found conversation with them fascinating and inspiring. In the Saskatchewan village I have called home for the last twenty years, I have never found a single person to talk to about my reading interests. Several of the women I met had been to Canada and had loved it. One woman knew an old friend of mine from university days.

Conversations with women in Germany particularly, though also in Ireland, made me look at Canada differently. The women I met envied the wondrous landscape, particularly the Rockies, and told me how much easier it was for a woman to own her own home in Canada. I had always seen my old church as a substandard hovel that I lived in because I didn't make enough money to have anything better. It had never occurred to me to think of it as property and privilege.

Ireland was my next stop. I was excited to be in an English-speaking environment again, and to be done with the stresses of my rapid tour of Germany and the emotional roller coaster of my visit to Holland. It hardly mattered that my luggage took several more days to travel between Munich and Dublin than I did. There was such joy in my heart during my time in Ireland — beginning the moment my feet touched Irish soil.

I fell head over heels in love with Ireland. I don't know what it was about the landscapes of the south of Ireland that moved and nourished me so much, or why I responded so strongly. Perhaps, because I have lived in a drought-blasted prairie landscape for so long, it was the stunning green I saw everywhere. Or perhaps it was the accessible scale of a land dotted with villages within walking distance of each other, a sense of community without being hemmed in, that I felt particularly drawn to. I also loved the musicality of the language and the warmth of the people I met. While Holland had nurtured me in many ways, in Ireland I felt that my spirit had found a home.

My first reading was in Dublin. After the reading, I saw a group of women clustered in one part of the room who seemed to be waiting until everyone else who wanted to speak to me had left. Their conversation among themselves was quite excited, and I thought that perhaps they were friends visiting each other and that this had nothing to do with me, so I prepared to leave.

Instead, I heard an astounding history. This was a group of sisters, their mother and their sisters-in-law who had come together to listen to me. Their family constellation of seven sisters and four brothers was quite similar to mine, which immediately interested me. One of the sisters-in-law had heard a child-abuse disclosure from a young niece that had shocked her. She had called one of the sisters in her husband's family and then, like dominoes falling, the story had begun to unfold. The father in this large family had been systematically preying on the children: his daughters, his nieces and his granddaughters. No one, until then, had ever told. The family figured out that this man had at least thirty-five victims they knew about in his long history as a pedophile. The women decided that they had endured enough, and together, as a family, they pressed criminal charges. Their mother left her husband and moved in with a daughter.

Throughout the trial, the father appeared certain that he would not be found guilty on any of the sexual-assault charges. He pleaded his age, ill health and, according to the report I heard from the sisters, appeared not to take the situation at all seriously. It was a gruelling trial for the family, but the evidence they gave before the court proved overwhelming. The father was found guilty and sentenced to seven times seven years in prison, the terms to be served concurrently. Family members were elated. Here was justice such as they had barely let themselves hope for.

Two weeks after the sentencing, when I returned to Dublin, they were still in a celebratory mood and invited me to a party. Meeting this family was very emotional for me, for I learned that there was a way to get an abuser convicted: what you needed was testimony and support from mother, sisters, cousins and nieces. This was not something I believed would ever be possible in my situation, but it felt exhilarating to know that it was possible at all. I am still grateful to this family for their hospitality and encouragement. I think of them often and hope that their healing path is a smooth one.

In Canada, women were very open with me about their experiences, whether on radio and television programs or during public events, whereas, in Europe, disclosures were rare and conversations about child abuse much more general. The focus in Europe was on child abuse as a societal problem, and government response to it, rather than on child abuse as a personal issue. In Ireland, the situation was different yet again. I spoke on a national radio program. It seemed an innocuous hour to me, filled with generalizations rather than graphic stories of incest. Yet everywhere I went in Ireland I was severely criticized for speaking about incest on the radio. "We don't talk about things like that here," the women said. Why not? "Because children might hear."

In Ireland, the issue of child sexual abuse was still very much hidden, and talking about it at all sometimes resulted in astonishing responses. In Canada, it seemed clear to everyone that men who abused must stop abusing. This didn't seem at all clear in many places I spoke in Ireland. After one reading, someone commented that women must become better at stopping men from abusing, an opinion held by most of the fifty women in the audience. This meant that they saw abuse as the responsibility of the women who were abused, and not of the perpetrators. There was a minority opinion voiced that this was the wrong approach and that men should understand that they had a responsibility not to abuse, period. A twenty-minute verbal free-for-all ensued, and I worried it would come to blows, so passionately did each woman feel about the position she believed was the right one.

I credit Emer Dolphin and the other women at Attic Press in Dublin for the fine quality of the time I spent in Ireland. With care and foresight, Emer organized my readings, bed-and-breakfasts and travel. She also drove me from Dublin to Galway, with stops for readings, fine dinners and sightseeing in Clonmel, Cork and Limerick. She answered my thousands of questions about Irish history and culture with patience and humour, and I felt that I could travel anywhere on the planet with her. I told her, when we got to Galway, that I just wanted to keep going, but of course she was expected back in Dublin. I think of Emer with great affection still.

After the reading tour was done, Emer helped me find a bed-and-breakfast in the vicinity of Galway in which I could spend the next ten days. Some were rejected out of hand because they were too close to a road for peace and quiet; others because they were filled with chatty or brash tourists. Eventually, we found the perfect place: Maureen and Colm O'Keady's house just outside Spiddal. Not only was it quiet and beautiful and off the road, but Maureen understood my allergies because her young son had nearly the same ones. I felt I was adopted for the duration of my stay. Here I rested for the first time in months, for there were no appointments to keep and no need to talk or think about child abuse. The ordinariness of family life and the comings and goings in the bed-and-breakfast were a great relief.

Maureen took me with her when she went to do errands in Galway, and on one memorable Sunday afternoon her in-laws gave me a glorious tour of the Connemara mountains in a bright red Porsche. On a particularly narrow stretch of road, the brand-new Porsche had its mirror nicked by a car travelling in the opposite direction. Both drivers stopped, almost a kilometre apart, and proceeded to scream at each other, though I doubt either of them could hear what the other said. When they had exhausted their shouting, they got back in their cars and continued on. I was reminded of my father and his fancy cars, any one of which had greater value than a child's life. A child could not go to a dentist to have a toothache treated, for that was expensive, but whatever the car needed was purchased, because that was important.

And then there was the fashion show. There was a government-sponsored project to encourage the women of County Galway to knit sweaters for the tourist trade, as knitting had all but died out in the area. Each woman who participated in the project was to bring her sweaters to a community hall to show them. There was a shortage of people willing to model the sweaters — although you couldn't tell that in the mayhem of the dressing room — so Maureen asked if I would show one of hers. I modelled a turquoise Aran-style sweater, and as I walked down the ramp of pushed-together banquet tables I was introduced in Gaelic: "Elly Danica, all the way from Canada," as though I had flown in specially for the event.

One day, with considerable trepidation because I don't like sea travel, I went by tour boat from Rossaveal to the island of Inishmore. On the wharf I hired a pony cart, shared with a German tourist because the driver said it was too expensive to ride alone, for the slow clipclop to the bottom of the hill on which sits the ancient stone fortress Dun Aengus. To reach the fortress you must first scramble over a defensive field of sharp stone spikes, not something that can be done with any dignity. Finally you reach the top of the hill and the double bank of stacked stone walls. There's a low doorway, through which even I had to stoop, and then you are within a half-circle, the open end of which is a sheer drop to the Atlantic Ocean. There is a massive stone platform in the middle of the site. I don't think I have ever seen the ocean from a more breathtaking spot. From the stone platform of Dun Aengus I looked toward the horizon. On the other side of this huge expanse of water, with rocks and some topography you'd swear were the same, lies Newfoundland.

I returned to Dublin in early June, and Emer and her friend Kathleen decided that they would show me some of the ancient sites along the Boyne River Valley. We began at Newgrange, where a tour of the passage grave takes all of ten minutes, and then out you go so the next group, usually a tour-bus load, can have their turn. The massive mound structure at Newgrange was built around 3200 BCE, which makes it older than the Egyptian pyramids. I found the power of this place awe-inspiring, and felt profound spiritual beliefs must have caused this enormous site to be built and decorated so beautifully all those ages ago.

We visited the remains of the mound at Dowth, then went on to Knowth, which has been stripped by archaeologists who have been studying it since 1962. Knowth looked more like a modern battlefield than anything else, so Kathleen suggested we go somewhere where we could get a better sense of what the mounds were really about. We drove to Slieve-na-Calliagh and clambered up a winding sheep path, which seemed to me to get ever steeper. The place to get the best view of the surrounding countryside is a huge carved and decorated curbstone called the Hag's Chair. To reach this viewpoint you scramble up the side of the mound and hoist yourself up onto the stone. All around are other hills with mounds on their summits, and it seemed possible to see all of Ireland from this vantage point. I felt, sitting there, that I was held in the hand of the Great Goddess.

Since my few moments perched on this great stone, I have read anything I can find about ancient Ireland and the goddess cultures of old Europe. What I seek is a connection to a culture or myth predating patriarchal society, in the hope that I can use this to think clearly about a social structure in which children and women are cherished members of society and treated with respect and honour.

The original plan for the tour called for me to travel on to England, but early on in my stay in Ireland, I realized that I was suffering from an exhaustion so intense that any further work or travel was impossible. The Women's Press, co-publisher of *Don't* in the U.K., had arranged publicity for me in England, and I was sorry to disappoint them but I could not continue after nearly six months of being on tour. With regret, I cancelled my trip to England and settled on the west coast of Ireland to await the day I could fly home.

After my travels in Ireland, I was anxious to get back to Canada. My life seemed to have changed so much since the publication of *Don't*, or perhaps I only hoped so. I was weary of travelling and yearned for a settled home so that I could get back to writing. I had hoped this home would be in the Maritimes, but financially it wasn't possible, so I went back to the prairies to sort out what had happened in the past eighteen months and decide what I wanted to do next.

Four

Redefining Family

    Family is in some ways the most difficult thing to write about. When I see the word "family" I have a difficult time relating to it, because it doesn't mean anything I want to think about. It should resonate with happy connections to a group of loving people who accept and cherish who I am and have struggled to become; the word "family" should be rich with nurturance and bonds with siblings. For me it means none of these things. Other people have families. I visualize a black hole where my family of origin ought to be.

    For all of us, family is the biggest hurdle in any effort to make disclosures of child abuse. Many disclosures founder or are retracted because of what the victim sees as the implications for her or his family. What is at stake is always how we see ourselves. Our personal identity is rooted within the concept of family, and disclosure could and often does mean the victim's banishment from the family and a resulting crisis in the sense of self.

Everywhere I read from *Don't*, I was asked about my relationship with my family. The questions from the women who came to hear me read were urgent and painful: What will become of my relationship with family members? Will they hate me, trash me, sue me, hurt me? How will they react? How will their reaction feel to me and what impact will it have on my life?

I would be sitting behind a table, signing books, a long line of women waiting their turn to speak to me. I would ask each woman what her name was so I could personalize the signing. And, as I handed the book to her, she would take my hand and tell me of her pain, saying she had never been able to tell anyone of the child she bore when she was thirteen, of the years of abuse by father, grandfather, uncle or neighbour. And how, she asked, was she to talk to her family about all this?

We must each weigh these questions with our own heart; there are no recipes for gaining specific hoped-for outcomes. In the best of all possible worlds, we would be taken into the bosom of our families and comforted. The abuser would be forced to leave the family constellation, and the rest of us would live happily ever after. While I did occasionally hear stories from women that followed some version of this path, they were rare.

Nevertheless, many women came to my speeches and readings with their sisters and their mothers and told me about the changes in their lives that occurred when they began to speak the truth about their childhood experiences. Some stories were especially memorable. One woman read my book, called her mother and her sisters and told them they had to read it, and within a very short time the burden she had carried alone for so long lightened as her family rallied in support of her. She said that where there had been silence for many years, her sisters and her mother were now talking honestly, supporting one another, and the future looked much brighter. That woman came to tell me the most profound of all things a writer can hope to hear: Your book has changed my life!

While I was travelling to promote the book and meeting women who shared their stories of childhood with me, I often said they were my family. Several years later, living once again isolated and alone, I don't have any sense of family that feels good to me. Whether this is a function of my history or of something else, I have yet to discover. What begins as defensive action, keeping to myself, ends up as an entrenched habit that is difficult to change.

❖ ❖ ❖

Early on, I had two roles in the family: one was little mother and the other was scapegoat. As the eldest of ten children I did an amazing amount of housework, child care and looking after my mother when life became too much for her to bear. Twice before I was fifteen, my mother had a nervous breakdown and went back to Holland to visit her mother while I looked after my nine siblings, the household and my father, and still tried to function at school. I used to say I had had my kids before I even left home, meaning that I had spent so much exhausting time looking after my mother's children that I wasn't about to give birth to any of my own.

I never felt like a child in relation to my mother, but like a smaller adult, a household servant with too much responsibility. None of the kids at school did anything like what I did in a day, and my requests for time to play were usually refused — my mother couldn't spare me for more than a few minutes at a time, and I tried to use that time to read.

My father never lifted a finger to help my mother with the daily round of tasks to keep ten kids washed, in clean clothing and fed. That was what Elly was for. If my mother was tired or distracted, it was my fault; I wasn't doing enough, and more tasks would be loaded on my young shoulders. I didn't mind helping my mother. I loved her and it was obvious that somebody had to help. What I minded was the abusiveness and the climate of fear of the father that shrouded everything in that household.

Because I was a pseudo-parent to my siblings — telling them what to do and making sure they did it — it was difficult to bond with my sisters and impossible to have anything like a healthy relationship with my oldest brother, who, at the whim of my father, was given my share of what food there was. This was further complicated by my father's insistence that everything I did was to be reported to him in detail so he could decide if punishment was necessary. I couldn't confide in or speak openly to anyone in the household. What I thought or said was always wrong, bad, ridiculous, stupid and reported verbatim to my father. Once, during a meal, when I disagreed with him about a high-school football score, he began to scream at me. When I wouldn't back down and say he was right, he threw a plate at my head. I ducked and the plate hit the wall behind me.

Laurie, the youngest of my siblings, was born when I was thirteen. Her childhood, I thought and hoped, would be very different from mine, for my mother had an intense bond with her youngest child, which I hoped meant she would protect her. I should have known better. Before Laurie was born I had tried, unsuccessfully, to warn my sisters about my father, but they had been well taught by him to discount everything I said. They had expressed amazement when I suggested that they should stay away from him and never under any circumstances spend time alone with him, especially not in his photography studio. They believed that the problem was with me and had nothing to do with him. It was folly to believe the pattern of abuse would be any different with Laurie. I wanted more than anything to leave my father's house, but I was anxious about the fate of my sisters and it was heart-rending to think of leaving them behind.

I look around me, especially during holidays, and envy every indicator of family I see: a mother and daughter shopping for clothes, a father and daughter laughing in a music store, sisters having lunch together and talking about their kids. The normal and ordinary things that families, and especially sisters, do are so far beyond my experience or dreams, and I can only look on in wonder. I mourn the loss of my nineteen nieces and nephews, most of whom I don't know and some of whom I have never met. I wish for family gatherings and meals, especially at Thanksgiving and Christmas. I dream of summer picnics. Most of all I miss my sisters.

As adults, my sisters tolerated me, but that was it. I had divorced a perfectly good husband, I lived in a dirty horrible old church, my new significant other was Jewish and my lifestyle was entirely too weird. My father didn't like the way I was living, so my life and concerns, according to my sisters, were as ridiculous as he so often said they were. They sneered at my poverty and pain and made fun of them, but prior to the publicity surrounding *Don't*, whenever my sisters were in trouble or distressed, they called on me for comfort.

I'm not sure what I expected to happen once the family became aware of the book. It had been rumoured among them for some time that I was writing, but I was careful not to tell anyone what subject I was exploring. When I received the offer to publish, part of my agreement with gynergy books was that no one would be told about *Don't* until it was actually out in the world. I think I probably harboured a bit of hope that my family would never hear of the book; they paid scant attention to any other aspect of my life. I knew it was more likely that, with the publication of the book, what little contact I still had with the family would end. Since I felt that all I got from these people were put-downs, abuse and misery, I thought I'd be better off if I didn't have anything more to do with them. I never for a moment believed that anyone in the family would accept my disclosures as true; still less did I expect any offer of comfort or support.

If the publication of *Don't* had any positive effect in regard to my family, it was that I was able to let go of the illusion that they cared about me in any way. Contact with my mother in the years before the book was published had been sporadic, and I almost never saw her alone. My parents sat side by side in matching armchairs in the living room of their house. Whatever my mother wanted to do had to be done where my father could see it. She didn't go to another room, even for a few minutes, without hearing him demand to know what she was doing. She didn't take a phone call he didn't listen in on, she didn't visit with anyone unless he was there. She sat in her chair, silent, doing embroidery or oil paintings: still life with tyrant. By the time *Don't* was published, my mother had been diagnosed with cancer, although the disease was, as far as I knew, still in its early stages, and she continued to live at home with my father.

Once *Don't* began to have wide distribution, there were some immediate implications for my parents. I heard these things in snippets from my sister-in-law, Linda, who is married to the oldest of my three brothers, and who would give me information about the family from time to time. According to her, my mother and father received threatening and abusive phone calls and were cut cold by people on the street and in local businesses. My father, eye on the main chance, apparently consulted a lawyer friend of his about suing me for a share of the royalties, since the book so patently told his story. The lawyer is said to have told him to keep his head down while he still could.

As news about the book spread, I got phone calls from two of my sisters, one in Italy, the other in Norway. One sister accused me of killing her mother (we never could say "our" mother; since none of us got what she or he needed from Mother, we could not, even in conversation, share her). I was appalled by the accusation and suggested that cancer was killing our mother. "No, no, you don't understand what this will do to her." "What about what was done to me?" "You're strong. You can deal with it. This will kill Mom. And besides, nothing like you say ever happened." "And what about your childhood?" I asked. "My childhood was beautiful, beautiful," she said.

Another sister phoned to demand why, if I had to write such shit, I didn't at least wait until my mother was dead. It wouldn't have made any difference, I said; then you would have accused me of besmirching her sacred memory. This will kill Mom, I heard again. I was accused of making a big grab for money, of being stupid, of being put up to this by a wily publisher.

Not one of my siblings has ever accepted or listened to anything I said. Why am I always, according to them, wrong and stupid? Why, even as adults, do they — without any examination of what they have been told — absolutely believe their father and refuse to hear me? The only explanation that makes any sense to me is that they are still in his thrall, and that it is fear and denial that keep their backs turned toward me. For if they acknowledged what happened to me, they would have to look at what happened to them. Unfortunately for me, they have to do that on their own agendas, not on mine, and that at least I can accept. I know too well how fierce denial can be, and I no longer have much investment in the hope that one day I will have healthy and vital relationships with my sisters. It saddens me to write this, but there it is.

In the last eight years, my sister Lucy, who lives in Norway, has visited twice and called once, while another sister, who lives in Moose Jaw, has spoken to me a few times when I met her accidentally in public or phoned her, and the other three sisters still have not spoken to me. My youngest sister, Laurie, had been killed in a car accident just after her twenty-first birthday.

My middle brother, I have not heard from. The youngest, I spoke to at his workplace when I was in the town where he lives, doing research for a project. The oldest brother tolerates me because his wife, Linda, is supportive of me, but he will not spend time with me unless it is to do maintenance work on my computer, and then Linda must be with him. He will not discuss anything except computers, period. I will not recant to suit the comfort level of my siblings, and it seems that, unless I do so, there will be little contact between us.

❖ ❖ ❖

In the fall of 1988, before *Don't* began to receive attention in Moose Jaw, I thought I had better find a way to see my mother. This was a complex and difficult thing to do. She was never alone, and any access to her was monitored carefully by my father. It wasn't even possible to talk to her on the phone without him listening in on the extension. I don't know what I thought I was going to do once I did see her, whether I'd tell her of the book or not.

When my mother went into hospital for tests related to her cancer, I phoned my sister who lives in Moose Jaw to find out when my father visited, because I didn't want to see him and wanted time with my mother alone. As it turned out, it didn't make any difference. My mother complained at length during my short visit about the parents of a son-in-law who treated her as though she were somehow lower class. My mother had worked hard all her life to help her husband struggle up the social ladder in Moose Jaw. This was a species of insult that made her very unhappy, because, even though she'd married beneath her European social standing, she most definitely knew she was not lower class. I realized, listening to her, that I had nothing to say to her, and she wouldn't let me speak anyway. I realized too, as I stood beside her bed, that I had come to say goodbye. I did not articulate my goodbyes, but though she lived for another two years, only twenty minutes away from my house, that was the last time I saw my mother.

What I had hoped — my most secret hope — was that, when she saw my book, my mother would do two things: acknowledge me as her daughter, and acknowledge the abuse and the horrors of my childhood. I never heard either of these things from her, but I didn't give up on that hope until she died. Somehow, I thought that things might change: that she'd see me as a person, tell me how sorry she was that I had had such a bad time, and finally turn her back on the man who had used her daughters in these horrible ways. I should have known better, of course, for — according to Linda — with her dying breath she was still taking care of her husband, smoothing his shirt front and straightening his tie.

My mother used to say that what she feared most was being alone in old age. I remember asking her how, with seven daughters, she could be worried about ending up alone. She said I didn't understand. She excused my father many things, she said (such as spending her retirement savings on stereos, computer equipment and cars), so she wouldn't lose him and be alone. And then life and fate never gave her an old age.

In November 1990 a friend called and read me my mother's obituary as it appeared in the Moose Jaw paper. I was not listed among her surviving children. None of my siblings had called to tell me she was close to death, though sisters had flown from Europe to be at her bedside. I learned from Linda that my siblings spent the two days before the funeral arguing about what they would do should I appear; my oldest brother assured them I would not be there. And I wouldn't have gone but for the obituary, which infuriated me, and the fact that not one of my siblings had called to tell me that Mother was on her deathbed.

I went to the funeral with a bodyguard consisting of two friends and the father of one of them. My friends timed our arrival so that everyone else was already seated in the funeral-home chapel. We sat toward the back, with me in the middle of the row. It was a wretched hour, not because it was my mother's funeral, but because it made clear how few friends she had of her own (a couple of women from her workplace), and because all in a row behind the family sat my father's cronies. The minister hired for the occasion spoke at length about a man who crossed Niagara Falls on a high wire, without ever making a point or linking his story to my mother's life. The whole thing felt like a play from the theatre of the absurd, including among the absurdities a sister who spent much of the time nibbling my father's ear lobe. I later heard two very disturbing things about the funeral. My father refused to pay for the funeral expenses and my middle brother covered the bill. And when asked by the funeral director what he wished done with my mother's ashes, my father told him to throw them in the garbage.

❖ ❖ ❖

A family history such as mine is poor training for motherhood. How was I to nurture a child when I had experienced so little nurturing myself? When I made my decision to leave my son in my husband's custody, that didn't mean I didn't want to see Greg as often as possible. I did not know then that my job description would be part-time mother. I found it all very confusing, as I'm sure Greg did too. Eventually he was old enough to tell me what he wanted to do when he visited with me, and he had a fine understanding of what was not possible because there wasn't money for it. We read a good deal and talked about books non-stop, even when he was small. Our absolute favourite activity was to spread newspapers over the table, find a roll of paper and paint big pictures.

I left my husband in 1972, and the divorce was final the next year. My ex-husband remarried within a couple of years. When Greg was eight, his family moved to Calgary; later they moved to Victoria. I saw him once a year if I was lucky: an occasional Christmas or a couple of weeks in the summer. Greg's memory and mine differ slightly about these times. I remember all I could not give him in so short a time; he, more generously, remembers what I did give him.

When we talked about this once, he said, "It was great. It was like there was nobody else in the world but me, and you have the best toys of any mom I know." He certainly had my undivided attention during his visits, for every year he was a new person I had to learn about. I also think it was great fun for him to have the run of my weaving and painting studio, with a chance to try everything that interested him.

In July 1988, when Greg was seventeen, I sent him a copy of *Don't*. I called to ask him first if I could do that, if he'd want to read it. Without hesitation he said, "Of course." The day he received the book in the mail, he sat down to read, and when he was finished he called me, weeping over what he had read. I will never forget what he said to me: First he assured me that he now understood clearly why I had not been able to look after him when he was small, and he thanked me for loving him enough to protect him from the pain I carried; then he said, "Not only does your father owe you for what he did, but he owes me, because he stole my mother." He also told me how proud he was of me. In 1990, Greg came to my reading in Victoria and sat in the front row of the auditorium, amazed by the mother he now saw as a public person.

I did not know what to expect when Greg read the book. I had told him very little about my childhood, as I didn't think it was appropriate to burden him with my pain. It was difficult enough to try to explain why I didn't live with him and why I couldn't afford to see him more often. I trusted that Greg had a good and generous heart, but the book was very painful, and I couldn't be sure how it would affect him.

When Greg was young, I occasionally took to him to visit my parents. I was careful to never let him out of my sight during the hour or so of my visit. Over the years, Greg used to ask me about the strange behaviour he had seen his grandfather engage in, which Greg couldn't understand. Why had my father been so interested in giving a twelve-year-old child pornographic magazines, as though it was normal to give such things to a child while his mother looked on? I curtly told my father to put the magazines away and, with a smirk that implied I was a prude, he would slide them back into the pocket of his chair. Why, when I was so poor and my father knew we had nothing to eat, had there never been an offer of dinner? Why had my father ordered my mother about as if she were a servant, tapping his cup against the saucer when he wanted something? What was wrong with the guy, Greg had wanted to know.

When I asked Greg to give me some thoughts about his response to *Don't* for this book, he wrote:

> *It was difficult dealing with the warring emotions of pride in your accomplishment, anger at [my grandfather], and sadness for what he had done to your life. On one hand I wanted to tell everyone, "Look at my mom; she came through this, she's a hero," and on the other hand it was like, I didn't want to be saying, "Look at my mom, she was abused," like it was some kind of freak show ... I felt immensely relieved that finally you'd got this canker out of your system and we could go back to trying to be a mother and son again without the grim spectre of your childhood hanging between us like the Sword of Damocles. It's a little selfish, I know. But it was like I'd finally got my mom back out of a prison that she'd been doing a life sentence in.*

We had time during the winter of 1990 to talk about the book and what it meant, and I believe it changed our relationship for the better. I think there is a deeper trust between us as a result of my openness about my experiences. In May 1995 my son married. Eliza Eisenhauer is everything a feminist mother could want for her son. She's strong, self-assured, determined. She is a truly warm and delightful young woman. Greg and Eliza live in Florida, which seems, from my desk in this small prairie village, very far away. My dreams of family have us living closer, at least in the same province. But in the latter years of the twentieth century, that's a dream that remains unrealized for many parents.

❖ ❖ ❖

Several factors in my life have worked against the creation of a wide network of friends who might have stood in place of my lost family. It is possible that, as an immigrant child, bookish, odd, sad and depressed, and further distanced by the abuse I was experiencing, I made isolation a habit. High-school friends became targets for my father, so it was too dangerous to have any girlfriends. He had told me it was my responsibility to have only friends he approved of — in other words, beautiful young girls who were potential prey.

The years of living alone, poverty and further bouts of depression kept me isolated as an adult. Once *Don't* was published, I withdrew farther into myself, for it was too exhausting and painful to hear the disclosures of other women wherever I was recognized. I go to town now with a clear sense of purpose: buy groceries, go to the library, keep my head down and get home as soon as possible.

In the early 1970s, at a weaving workshop, I met a woman who was to have a profound and enduring impact on my life. Her name was Kate Waterhouse and, when I met her, she was over seventy years old. She had an incredible passion for life and anything to do with weaving, spinning, working with vegetable dyes, and politics.

Kate invited me to visit her home, which I did as often as I could, travelling by bus or borrowed van the ninety minutes to where she lived. Each time I visited, she welcomed me with food specially prepared because she knew I liked it. She would make muffins and breads out of rice flour to accommodate my allergies. She told me that a proper visit required I stay for lunch and supper.

Kate's kitchen was an oasis for me during many difficult years, for here we would talk about the state of the world, our weaving projects and our lives. The room was always crowded with her projects: two looms, a spinning-wheel, a table covered with recipes and articles clipped from newspapers and magazines, and her various recycling projects.

I came to Kate's kitchen to hear her stories of pioneer days in Saskatchewan, to discuss politics, to exchange weaving books and information, and to share jokes. More than this, I came to bask in the love and generosity she lavished on me.

Kate was born in 1899 to Irish parents near Winnipeg. After her mother died when she was small, she was raised in the city by a grandmother who was a midwife. Life was not easy for Kate. She once said that she did not own the labour of her own hands until she was over sixty. She had beautiful hands that were rarely still, and she worked hard to make beauty blossom out of everything she touched. She took care over, took pains with, everything she did. She wasted nothing.

Kate taught me much: how to cook for one, how to put up and freeze food and make jellies and jams. She loved her garden, and over many years she taught me how to grow vegetables and herbs. When she was over ninety, she and her daughter came to visit, bringing trees she had started from seed in styrofoam cups, a crab apple and a mountain ash, each barely ten centimetres tall. For once I didn't lose them as soon as I planted them. The ash is now taller than I am and the crab apple is nearly as tall. My yard contains rosebushes started from suckers Kate had me dig out of her garden, two pink and a yellow. I have irises and daisies, gooseberries, a plum tree and winter onions, all from Kate's garden.

In the last years of her life, each time I said goodbye after a visit she gave me a kiss and told me she loved me. In her late eighties Kate called once and asked me to come for a three-day visit. She had something she wanted to tell me. For those three days we told stories about what we meant to each other and thanked each other for gifts and all the time we had shared. It was, I realized later, our time to say our formal goodbyes, and it was a very beautiful experience. Several months before she died, Kate asked her daughter to call me with a message: to tell me she loved me. Kate's love and all she taught me will continue to sustain and inspire me.

Apart from Kate, there have been other sustaining friendships in my life, and by far the most enduring one is with Barry. Barry Lipton came into my life twenty-three years ago, while we were both students at the University of Regina. For six years we lived together, and it was Barry who helped me move out of the city and into the old church I bought in the country. Early in our relationship I asked him for help with a project — and he's been helping me ever since.

Without his steadfast, generous financial and emotional support, it would be much more difficult for me to spend time writing.

Our friendship has survived many changes in both our lives. Barry moved from Regina to Toronto in 1988 and married Daina Green in 1995. Even though it is now nearly seventeen years since he and I lived together, I think he still knows me better than anyone else, for he's seen me through so much: years of depression, illness and poverty, and then the personal triumphs of textile and painting shows and the publication of *Don't*. The older I get, the more I cherish a relationship with so much history. It wasn't easy to build a sustainable friendship after we stopped living together, but the effort it took was well worth it. We rarely see each other more than once or twice a year, but we talk on the phone several times a week. Nobody believes in me more or gives me more encouragement than Barry — his friendship is a treasure.

I'm learning that family need not be the collection of people into which you are born, but can consist of people to whom you choose to relate. It seems such a simple thing in some ways, but it is hard to give up entirely on one's family of origin. These were the companions of my childhood, and there seems to be a never-ending desire to be connected with them and to be acknowledged as a cherished member of this family. I don't suppose I can change that desire. It is, after all, in most circumstances a reasonable one.

Five

Reinventing
Myself

I'd like to be able to write a report from the magic kingdom where I was transported after *Don't* was published. I'd like to be able to say that I lived happily ever after with my new family, true love, art and fabulous riches, in a palace of great beauty. Alas, it isn't so. I may no longer see myself as Cinderella sitting beside the hearth, sorting out lentils from among the cinders, but I still have entirely too much of a sense of the little match girl looking in from the cold while others enjoy the party.

Many things changed after I wrote *Don't*, and more things have changed in the years since. I've certainly grown as a person. I'm stronger and even more fiercely determined than I was before. I still struggle with low self-esteem, and my frustration with the poverty and isolation of my life isn't any less. If anything, my frustrations are more intense, for now I have seen what else there is in the world and I yearn to participate.

It has taken time to sort out which of these too numerous frustrations are with residuals of childhood abuse and which are simply the result of being a woman and an artist in an economy and time that do not value either women or artists, and value still less women who are artists. I have during the last few years worked on several writing projects, until lack of money became overwhelming and sent me off on various detours designed to bring in income. The result was rarely much in the way of income, and sometimes an unfortunate hiatus in creative energies. This is the stuff of every artist's life. It isn't true that an artist makes better art when weighed down by worry and insecurity. This is a nice myth trotted out as justification by a culture determined to ignore an artist until she or he has been safely dead for at least one hundred years.

By 1990, the travel and work I was doing had begun to take a toll. I had been touring with the book on and off for eighteen months; I had travelled across Canada several times and spent seven weeks in Europe. I had completely run out of steam. All I wanted to do was sleep and stay in one place for more than three days. But I felt I should find some way to continue this work; the issue was so urgent. Many people I met while I was promoting *Don't* had suggested that I become a counsellor, and I had said I would think about it, for obviously the need was great; most counselling services were so overburdened with clients that the waiting period was two years or more.

The end of the promotion tour began a time of great ambivalence for me, one I don't think I have resolved to my satisfaction. I am a writer and an artist; writing and art are the work I want to do with my life. But I had made significant contact with a great many women with my book. What responsibilities did that entail? Should I abandon my artistic endeavours and go back to school to train as a counsellor? Should I write another book in the same vein? Was I entitled to the rest of my life or not? Was it my responsibility, as one reader so passionately put it, to help people feel better because my book had upset them so much?

And herein lay the real dilemma. Going back to my ordinary life meant going back to rural Saskatchewan and poverty, and I did not want ever to go back to living like that. If I trained as a counsellor, I could make a living, and perhaps do some good. Everywhere I went there was temptation to take that path, to make a living and to be of use. I was told that I had a way with people, that I offered comfort so well. One woman told me that her clients had benefited more from twenty minutes with me than from three months of therapy. Yet my inner resistance to doing this work was every bit as intense as the outside pressures steering me toward it, leaving me in a constant state of turmoil. I began calling myself names, accusing myself of not caring, even as I realized that I did care, very much. I simply wasn't sure that this was right for me, even though it would likely earn me a decent living because counsellors were in demand. So what, I asked myself, was I going to do for money instead?

In 1991, I received a grant from the Canada Council to write the first draft of an ambitious fiction project. Wrestling with this project was, as is always true for me, intense and physical. Some writers, I've heard (though who has met any?), are fortunate in that things come easily to them. Life, at least my life, doesn't work that way. It took me from 1973 to 1987 to write *Don't*, of which thirteen years and ten months were spent sorting it all out. If I need to produce two books a year to make a living as a writer, I have obviously got a long way to go — and I have my doubts whether I even want to achieve this level of production.

Once the grant money was gone, what I should have done was stay at my desk and keep writing, no matter what was unravelling around me. Instead, to keep some income coming in, I agreed to undertake various speaking engagements. At first I was grateful for the opportunity to spend time away from my desk. My writing project wasn't going well anyway, so I thought I would do what I could to educate the public about child abuse, see something of the country and earn some money.

I spoke at conferences twice a year for the next four years. It was while I was composing my first speech that I made the transition from speaking personally to speaking politically. I wanted to see beyond my own story, beyond individual victims and perpetrators, to the social and political causes of child sexual abuse. I read social

and psychological theory and many of the books then being published about the issue.

To find the courage to make this transition from a personal to a
more overtly political voice, I wrote more than two hundred pages
of arguments with myself about why I should or should not do this.
The idea of taking a stand and possibly being wrong was nerve-
wracking. After all, during a speech, there is nobody at the podium
but me, and I am not representing any political views other than my
own. Now, there's loneliness for you!

For a time I thought that speaking on child-abuse issues was my
life, and that my writing and painting projects should be abandoned
in favour of this mission I had fallen into. I certainly could not
combine the two. To speak for one hour cost me a minimum of
three months away from my writing. There was the usual struggle
to get the speech written on time, followed by weeks and weeks of
exhaustion caused by the intensity of the experience of meeting
survivors and those dedicated to helping them. Responding com-
passionately to so many stories and lives filled with pain required
that I spend many weeks afterwards processing what I had heard
and trying to understand it.

Now, as I think back on it, in the three years after my mother's
death, when I avoided and otherwise tried to outrun my sorrow, it
helped to have a justification for staying away from personal writing
or any engagement with my feelings. The speeches were one way of
doing this; then there were the projects I undertook between the
spring and fall conference seasons. One summer I decided to
drywall the basement, the next I read hundreds of mystery novels,
the one after that I designed a life-writing correspondence course
that never found any clients. Perhaps it was important to do these
things. It is only when I look at my unfinished writing projects that
I wonder.

Avoidance never works for me for very long, and in January 1993
I ran full tilt into a serious illness. I wonder why all my crisis points
revolve around physical illness; is that the only time I'll pay attention? Probably. This time, though, I think the sheer weight of what
I had been carrying for five years simply bowled me over. I knew I

was exhausted and should quit all public-speaking engagements and rest. But, I argued with myself, if I quit, how will I eat and pay the bills? How can I go on without any money?

I spent a month in hospital while the doctors drained my lungs, did exploratory surgery and tried to come up with a diagnosis. I lost sixteen kilograms and looked awful. For that month I hardly ate or slept. I thought I was dying, and I looked it. It was clear that I was not getting better in hospital but progressively worse. So I picked up the phone in Regina and called Barry in Toronto: "Barry, I need you." That was at nine o'clock in the morning; by nine that evening he was at my bedside. He took one look at me and knew exactly what to do. I needed vitamin supplements and fresh food, he said; so he brought me meals: little green salads and poached fish he made in a friend's kitchen. As soon as I had something tempting that I could eat, I began to rally. When you have as many food allergies as I have, it is nearly impossible to get anything approaching nutrition from an institutional kitchen.

And then 1993 was such a bad year to be ill. The Canadian Federation of University Women's group in Saskatoon had been trying for three years to organize an event at which I could be invited to speak, and I didn't want to let them down. In April I was to speak at a conference in Kelowna, and the next day I had to fly across the continent for a painting show and speaking engagements in Newfoundland. And then I was offered a seasonal job as a book rep, which meant I had to be at the Learned Societies conference in Ottawa in May. It wasn't the right time for any of these things, but I wasn't going to let that stop me.

I left the hospital against the advice and wishes of the doctors. They had done a bronchoscopy and wanted to do more exploratory surgery; I wanted to finish the paintings for the show in Newfoundland and do the things I had planned for the spring. I thought that considering my condition — I weighed all of forty-four kilograms — more surgery was not a wise idea. My lungs had ceased filling with fluid, the drain hoses had been removed and there was a tentative diagnosis of sarcoidosis: a rare chronic disease of unknown cause that affects the lungs, organs, bones and skin.

I gave myself a week or so to rest, and then I went to the painting table and got busy. Once the paintings had been sent to Newfoundland, I began work on the speeches. I had a couple of weeks to get myself together and strong enough to give the speech I had promised in Saskatoon, though I didn't know how I would find enough breath to speak for an hour. Then I had a couple of weeks after that to rest up before another hectic six weeks away from home.

By early June I collapsed again. The book-rep job required that I work with new books and catalogues, and I discovered that I was highly allergic to fresh printer's inks. What tolerance I had once had to such allergens was gone as a result of the sarcoidosis. Unhappily I had to give up the book-rep job. I managed to drag myself home, and then spent the summer so exhausted I could barely make myself a meal. Still, I didn't think I had to give up the speaking engagements planned for October.

A series of readings and speeches were planned for southern Alberta, in Cardston, Pincher Creek, Lethbridge and Calgary. I didn't anticipate any problem. I thought I was reasonably well. But no sooner did I leave home than I got a ferocious attack of shingles on my midriff and nearly all the way around my back. In Calgary I stayed with my oldest brother and his wife, Linda. Linda, watching me try to ignore the pain, took things in hand. I was supposed to be part of a panel discussion at a conference one morning, but when one of the organizers came to pick me up for the drive across Calgary, Linda said, "No, she can't go. I'm taking her to the doctor." The doctor said the usual things: This was serious; she hadn't seen a case like this outside Eastern Europe; cancel everything, go home and rest. What? Me? Disappoint people? No way. Besides, if I didn't speak I wouldn't earn the money to pay my bills, most particularly my property-tax arrears, and then where would I be? So I finished my engagements bent double in pain. What a trooper! What an idiot!

I knew I would have to stop the travel, at least for a while, and spend some time reconnecting with the rest of my life. It wasn't that I travelled all the time, it was just that I hadn't given myself enough time to recover from the exhaustion generated by the physical crisis at the beginning of the year. I promised myself that I would not actively seek further engagements, and would do only what I had already promised. There was nothing scheduled between the end of October and the spring of the following year. The spring of 1994 was hectic, but I was much stronger and had less trouble coping with the schedule.

One of the most difficult things I had to do was find a way to look after myself physically. I have always felt that my body is a more or less useful support for my head, and I have paid as little attention to it as possible — except, of course, when I was ill. I was beginning to feel there was something to be said for more positive attention to the needs of my body. A friend in Moose Jaw suggested I see a massage therapist she knew of, but I kept postponing the visit, even though I was making little progress in recovering from the tendonitis that had developed in both arms when I overdid one of my money-making schemes. I had collected bulrushes in roadside ditches for basket making. Weaving little rushwork baskets and mats was fun but hard on my hands, for I worked twelve-hour days. Tendonitis, not income, was the unhappy result, and months later it was no better.

Finally I made an appointment to see a massage therapist, but only for a meeting so I could get a sense of whether I would feel comfortable working with her. She was understanding and talked to me about the healing techniques she practised: craniosacral therapy, reiki and massage. I found I liked her and her approach. She and her colleague began to work with me in the spring of 1995, and, in the year since, I have felt much better, both emotionally and physically. Often during treatments I experience intense emotional catharsis, as well as relief from the aches and pains in my shoulders and arms that are the result of sitting at a computer or painting most of every day. What I like about these treatments is that they involve only a very light touch, so nothing ever feels invasive or frightening to me.

It is now, as of this writing, two years since I've travelled much. During these two years I have spoken in Saskatoon at a memorial for the women who died in the Montreal Massacre and have given a reading in Peterborough, at Trent University. I think I have had my rest now. During this break from public speaking, I have spent much time and energy attempting to reinvent myself as a writer. I finished one fiction project, set aside a couple of others and began another. Wayne Schmalz, then a producer for CBC Regina, suggested that I write a radio play based on an excerpt of my novel in progress. This project was very enjoyable, and Wayne was wonderful to work with. *Jane's Story* aired on CBC Regina in June 1995.

Then it seemed necessary as part of my reinvention process to take a long look at what had happened to my life after the publication of *Don't*. No sooner had I written myself an outline for this project than the current publisher of gynergy books called me with a serendipitous offer of a book contract.

A writer probably reinvents herself with every book. I felt a particular need to reinvent myself because I knew only one way to write, and that was in great pain, primed for a life-and-death battle with the content and the words. I neither could nor wanted to live my entire writing life this way. I had to find a healthier way to write or give it up. I often seriously considered choosing the second, easier option. It isn't, however, a choice that would make me happy.

I continue to struggle intensely with a confusion and ambivalence about my responsibilities to child-abuse issues. It is physically, emotionally and spiritually exhausting to work in this field, and to do so without professional training and support does not make a lot of sense and could well do more harm than good.

In order for me to do such work effectively, I feel I would have to dedicate my life to it. And what would become of the writer and artist I am? To what do I owe the time and energy of my life if not to my creative work? And, yet, how can I not give absolutely everything to help change the world to make it safe and healthy for children? Is it better to make noble gestures or to be true to oneself? This is a moral dilemma I have by no means resolved.

Six

In Search of
My Mother

I am particularly haunted by my need to make peace
with my sense of my mother and with my own experience of mothering. What does it mean to "mother"? Who should do this work? Who,
in fact, does this work? And what, in the best of all possible worlds,
should mothering be, and give to the one doing the mothering and to
the one who receives it? Mothering is a gift that cannot be enforced or
demanded. It must be freely given or it is poisonous.

Most definitions of "mother" are empty of emotional content
and talk of "female parent," or "to give birth to," or "to protect as a
mother," or "to profess oneself the mother of a child." "Female
parent" is about as neutral a phrase as you can get. It doesn't carry
anything like the yearning and pain many of us have in our guts as
soon as we think of our mothers.

Yearning? Pain? Yes, there is pain in the image of mother. The
woman who was my mother is unknown to me. I know where she

lived, something of how she lived, but I know nothing of who she was as the woman who brought me into the world through her body.

"Mother" means abandoned. My mother abandoned me — not to life, when I was strong enough to fly my little path on my own, but raw, untaught, terrified and much too young. There were the usual reasons. She had a second child thirteen months after my birth, and a third thirteen months after my sister's birth, and a fourth and a fifth, until what she had was a brood of ten — each abandoned in her or his turn.

There are — I have heard of them — women who undertake the care of such large numbers of children with joy. My mother was not one of them. In her fierce struggle with poverty and endless pregnancy, she had nothing left to give her children. She gave us life, and then, exhausted, she abandoned us. I wonder how she survived her childbearing years. I wonder how any woman survives the stress of multiple pregnancies without time between to recover her physical strength; without time to know the infant she has brought into the world; without time to think about her own life.

What stays with you, always, is the yearning. I still yearn for mothering, though I am many years past the time when one would think it necessary. And I yearn for something much sadder than this: I yearn for the ability to mother the only child I brought safely into the world. For, not having received appropriate mothering, and understanding mothering as a hostile act (at least in my experience), I could not give this gift of mothering to my child. I would not do to my child what was done to me, though what that meant was that I abandoned him in a slightly different way. The only choice I thought I had, which I saw clearly then and see even more clearly now that I understand something of my past, was to abuse him or abandon him.

We have been fortunate, he and I. He grew strong and whole in safety. Another woman was able to give him what I could not. So, he tells me now, he has two mothers. And he no longer believes I left him to the care of his father and stepmother because I didn't love him enough to care for him myself.

He would come to visit me when he was little for that bizarre ritual that divorce forces on kids, the weekend. For a day and a half I would struggle to mother, as I tried to understand what that meant and what it required of me. He was patient, clever at pointing out areas where I didn't understand what he needed — though perhaps seeing the mess his "mother" was in caused him considerable confusion.

His visits always began with the same denial: "You're not my mother, you know. You weren't there when I was born. Mothers stay with their kids and do the work. You're selfish. You're not my mother." Half his pain, half his father's. So every visit began with a fight, as I — another needy child — in reaction to this onslaught-fought with my needy son about what it meant to be his mother. You can't explain adequately, to a six-year-old, why you can't be there for him, why it is much better for him that you are not.

And yet there was this: When we saw each other, even after long absence, when we could make eye contact, we knew who we were. He knew in his gut that I was his mother, just as I knew in my gut that this beautiful child was my son. The bond is not mythical; it does exist. It tugged us into a relationship, even when that relationship was fraught with pain, difficulty and denial.

❖ ❖ ❖

I wake today to thoughts of Demeter. Demeter is the goddess who was in so much pain at the loss of her daughter to the god of the underworld (the god of men) that she sat and wept and refused to allow the world to continue as it had before. Now there would be no more fertile fields; no animals would reproduce to provide food.

Demeter's reaction to the rape of her daughter is written of in many ways, to support all kinds of ideas of how goddess imagery functions for women. I too have my ideas about this: I see a woman so devastated that she knows not only that the world will never be the same for her or for her daughter, but that she has the power to make it different. During the time when she knows her daughter must be in the underworld, Demeter removes fertility from the fields. The time when she must think about, feel, the pain of her daughter in the underworld is winter, when all the world is made to share her bleak sorrow.

Some part of me responds with: Yes, I know this is how it feels to have your child abducted and raped. This is what I would have wanted my mother to feel and do: to know that the world could not go on in the old ways, that things were changed for us, utterly changed. And then I would have wanted her to take the most profound and dramatic action she could think of to have me returned to her safekeeping.

Of course, this means I assume several things. I assume, in this scenario, that my mother is strong. I assume that my mother, like Demeter, has the power to effect her wishes and decrees. I assume that she would know and care with her whole being about what happened to me and would take immediate action both to rescue me and to punish the perpetrators.

In fact, I grew, as an adult, to see that my mother had little power. She certainly did not have the power adult men exercise so readily and with such devastation. And all through my childhood and well into my later years, and perhaps still, I ask the same question: Why? Why did my mother not have the power to stop the abuse of her children?

We hear more and more about how women have primary responsibility to protect their children. Women are now being charged in conjunction with the perpetrators of sexual assault. And I worry that this is an indication of where society wants to take the sexual-assault issue. It is so much easier to blame Mom. The abuser, well, "he never did nothin' to the kid." So Mom's right there again, powerless and victimized with her children.

One wonders how long we'll allow the abuser, society and the courts to sentence a mother for not doing what the abuser and society have made it impossible for her to do. Never provided with the resources to protect her children or herself, she will now be sentenced for failing to give protection.

It is not just physical resources that she lacks — proper housing, adequate support money (whether from the state or from the father/husband). The resources necessary to enable a woman to be strong enough to protect her children are not merely financial, though I certainly don't want that factor underestimated. What every child needs from birth is respect and caring for who she or he is, and for the child's integrity as a human being. And then each child needs a nurturing environment, encouragement to grow in strength and in health, and empowerment to act as an adult.

Until we have women who are empowered to act, first on their own behalf as children and young women, and later as protectors and nurturers of children, patriarchy has no business throwing women in jail for not doing what society has made sure they cannot do. This is no different from blaming the child for the abuse. And it quite nicely erases the guilt and responsibility of male perpetrators.

Politically, then, I am not able to blame my mother. Yes, she knew what was going on. Yes, she should have protected me. Yes, yes, yes, I wanted her to help me. But in the context of her time and place and personal background, and her relationship with her husband, she was powerless. I saw that clearly after the first time he abused me. At first she believed me; then I watched him make her choose between her husband and her daughter, and I saw that she felt her only option was to choose him and sacrifice me. We should not be surprised — outraged, certainly, but not surprised.

What is it that makes it more important for a woman to believe her husband than to listen to her child? Let's get something clear right away. She assumes that if she chooses to believe the child, her husband will either hurt her or leave her; if she chooses to believe him, she will be (in this bizarre scenario) rewarded in that he will become his sweet and charming self again, for a time. Probably he will tell her to forget it; it's over and they can get on with their lives. She may even receive a present of some sort — a night out, new clothes or jewellery. Things will, she hopes, get back to normal.

Women told me of having to make heart-rending decisions in this scenario. Too often, if a woman chooses to believe, support and protect her child against her husband, he will become enraged and punitive. He'll take the car and he'll leave, calling her every name he can think of to hurt her, beating her up once more just to prove to her that he can hurt her more than she can hurt him. And she and her children will be without any financial support or resources, and often without a place to sleep. Make no mistake about it, she knows this. It is part of every fight she has with the man she lives with — "If I push him, he'll leave." And she sees in her mind's eye what that will mean to her. And don't mistake this, either: he knows she knows, and that is his power over her — "She's not going to leave. Where will she go? She's got nothing, no car, no money, nothing."

As an adult I don't blame my mother for not leaving. It makes no sense to rail at her or to hate her for what she couldn't do. Once, when I complained particularly bitterly to her (I was thirteen), she made the issue clear: "I have nine other kids besides you. If he leaves, we'll starve." How could I argue? I knew it was true, knew we barely had enough to live on even with his support. I offered to work to support the family in his stead, told her I thought we could do it together. But she dismissed the idea and told me to do what he wanted. It was better for all of us, she told me, and, anyway, none of us had any choice. This was the way the world was. I learned a painful lesson that day from my mother — added to the many other childhood lessons in powerlessness, in hopelessness, and in the fact that a woman's life can be unremitting pain and humiliation — the lesson that we have no choice, ever.

Would this childhood, these lessons, have fitted me to raise a child? Would I have been able to protect my child? And is this not what patriarchal society asks of abused women: out of a childhood of powerlessness we must, upon giving birth, become powerful and take appropriate measures to see to the health and safety of the child? How would I or most other abused women know what is healthy, safe, appropriate for children, never having experienced it, and likely not even having seen it?

I was led to believe that my childhood was a normal one. That abuse of girls was normal. That my father was normal in his demands of me. That men use children and women. So how and why would I have learned to protect my future children from this normal behaviour on the part of their father? This doesn't make sense. If such behaviour is normal, then there is nothing to be done. But if it is not normal, what is? It will require a lot of work to find out, so that I can trust that my reactions are appropriate for the health and protection of my child.

Yet, society expects an eighteen-year-old abused woman with a baby and no support to know how to protect both herself and her child. And expects her to do that when she has stars in her eyes about love and her man. And expects she'll believe it when she is told he has the potential to hurt her or her child. Her man? He's not like that. She knows him better than that. He wouldn't hurt anyone. He's a good man, not like some of those other jerks out there.

And if he bashes the baby around (he didn't mean to, she knows that) because he's jealous, and wants to be and is her baby first, she is expected to understand this and take responsibility for it. She is expected, further, to know what's going on and what she ought to do. She has nothing (if she left, where would she go?) — just the life-and-death responsibility of protecting the baby from her man, who has changed so much since the baby was born that she no longer recognizes him for who she thought he was when they were courting.

❖ ❖ ❖

My mother never loved me. "Impossible," I hear you say as you read that. "Impossible," I say, joining with you in the hope it isn't true. I have always tried to tell myself that my mother loved me but that she didn't know, for some reason, how to show me that she did. I have clung to this dream secretly, surely, against all evidence to the contrary.

I remember a time, long ago, when I did not doubt that my mother loved me — a golden age of being enveloped in her caring, of basking in a trust in the world and in my mother that had no boundaries. Was this ever true, or was it a myth I clung to to keep me sane?

My memories are definite. There was a "before," when my mother loved me, and an "after," when she no longer loved me. It seemed that it was my fault. If I had not told her what my father had done, if I had not reacted to his abuse but kept it locked away as he told me I must, my mother would not have had to choose between him and me — and, choosing him, no longer love me.

From that day she turned me to face her as she dried my back after the bath I had demanded after the first time my father abused me when I was four years old, I don't remember her ever touching me except to hit me. No hugs, no cuddles with a story before bedtime, no tucking me into bed with a good-night kiss. Nothing but an unrelenting dismissal — get out of my sight — and constant denial that I was her child. And yet I clung tenaciously to the hope well into my thirties that she loved me. How does one survive without this? If it was a myth, so much the better. Myths don't tarnish.

Each time I saw my mother I would explain away her behaviour in some way — she had had a bad day or night, she was stressed about money, her job was particularly gruelling that week — anything and everything I could think of to account for the fact that I meant nothing at all to her and I could read that in her eyes. Like a hungry puppy, I kept coming back. Feed me, feed me, love me, love me. And oh, how it hurt. Perhaps, even — wretched thought — it was the hurt I wanted. It was the hurt I knew, after all, from the time I was four. If my mother and I continued to operate as we always had, I was still connected to her. She was still my mother. As long as she was hurting me in the old ways, she was still my mother.

In desperation, I learned to build a wall — more than one, a fortress perhaps — between myself and feeling. Feeling hurts too much, feeling is only pain, and I simply could not take any more of that and expect to live. Feeling could push me over the edge and into a beyond where I could not survive. So feeling was the last thing I could or wanted to do.

After I got married and left home, my relationship with my mother took on a formal tone. We would meet only for a fifteen-minute coffee break, in a public place, a restaurant where confrontation of any sort was impossible. We were never alone; that would have been too dangerous. If we had been alone, my feeling and hurt and anger would have escaped the fortress built around them, and who knows what I would have said? So safely, for fifteen minutes, we discussed the weather, her health and, sometimes, the uncontrolled spending of her money by my father. And then she would leave to go back to work. She usually paid for my coffee, with the remark that I would never get my act together to be able to afford so much as a coffee in a restaurant. Out on the street we would say our formal goodbyes.

I used to sit in that restaurant and think that she could have exactly the same conversation with anyone else there. Most other women around us did a better job of feigning interest in each other. My mother never even tried. She endured those fifteen minutes with "what's her name" and then went back to the office. I can still see her, face pulled tight, her entire posture defensive, waiting, waiting. Waiting for what? Only once did I go beyond the bounds of our coffee-break contract. Once I tried to tell her of violence against children and women. Nothing specific, no references to our past. She gave me her hardest look and said, "Is that right?" The implication being clear — that I'd made this up too.

When I got home after seeing my mother, I would be miserably depressed, often for weeks. I didn't make the connection for a long time. I didn't want to see the relationship between my fantasy of a mother who cared about me and wanted to hear my news, whatever it was, and the woman who sat across from me in a restaurant once a month and endured my presence and conversation. Of course I was depressed. Here I was, so needy, literally begging this woman to acknowledge me in some way as her daughter, and I got nothing, nothing at all.

So no, my mother didn't love me. And now I think her sorrow must surely have been greater than mine. I have other women in my life who I know love me. What did she have? The man she had chosen, all those years ago, the man who was so much more important than her children that she always allowed him to stand between them and her. The love and understanding I had for my mother she never accepted, or perhaps even knew about.

The pain of yearning — pain for a different life, a different mother or even the mother she once was (in dream? myth? reality?). My healing demands that I accept her for who she was. My healing demands that I remove my fantasy mother and replace her with the woman who did not protect me, and who made it clear over and over again that she did not love me.

When I married and left my father's house, it was imperative that I become a mother — or so my husband told me. It is rape (many rapes) when you are made pregnant against your will. And how do you come to terms with a child conceived in rape? The first time I was pregnant, in the third year of my marriage, the fetus did not survive, and I was thankful. I knew that I was not able, not anything like ready, to care for a child. There was so much pain, so much felt wrong in my life. How could I drop or ignore all that and take responsibility for a child? I was still a child myself, a hurt and angry child.

This first pregnancy resulted in a miscarriage that set off nightmares when I had been free of them for some time. My nights were terror. During the day I wept and tried to write about how I felt. I could not function in a normal or healthy way, I was in so much pain. And I was very confused. If I was grateful that I had miscarried at five and a half months, why did I weep all day? I did not feel sorrow, I felt relief, so why could I not stop my tears?

My husband was alarmed by my behaviour, for I was either catatonic or in tears, and I couldn't explain any of it to him. And no, I didn't want another baby to make it better. I didn't want another baby ever. Those are fighting words to the patriarchy, so at that point something had to be done about me and my attitude. My husband decided I needed to see a psychiatrist to fix me up.

The psychiatrist looked exactly like photographs I have since seen of Papa Freud in his study. He sported a goatee and smoked a pipe. The office had ambient lighting, a couch and framed certificates of the psychiatrist's accomplishments on the walls. There were two matching boxes for tissues, one on the desk beside the armchair, one near the couch. He sat stiffly in a swivel chair. I was encouraged to use either the couch or the recliner; in either case I was to be as close to supine as possible.

From the first meeting with the psychiatrist in the office in which I was going to be fixed up, I was terrified. As soon as the door shut I felt trapped. As soon as I looked at him, the faces of men I did not remember or recognize superimposed themselves on his face. I could not keep him in focus. The faces of other men flashed by over and over again.

He wants me to talk about my problem. I don't have a problem, I say. I think my husband has a problem. He doesn't think I can work out what I need to work out by myself, doesn't trust that I know, deeply know, what I'm doing. My husband's problem is that he has run out of patience with me and my so-called problem. I realize the psychiatrist doesn't want to know about my husband's problem, but I try it anyway. With all this elaborate preparation for disclosures of some kind, something must be said in this room before I will be allowed to leave. That, at least, is immediately obvious.

He wants to talk about my mother. How can I even begin? How can I tell this creepy little man that I don't think I have a mother, but that there is a woman who won't claim me as her daughter because she says I'm too much of a trouble-maker. This is the woman I have grown to hate, and the hate is all mixed up with yearning for a mother who will love me. I don't understand what I've done (and I have hidden from myself almost all of what happened) that makes it impossible for her to love me.

And the psychiatrist, between puffs of thick smoke from his pipe, tells me that it will all be better when I have a baby. How can having a baby make it better? I ask. Because then you won't have time to think about these things, he says. I won't have time to think about it? I should just stop thinking? This is the advice of the psychiatrist: You won't have any problems if you stop thinking.

Oh yes, and he meant it, no doubt about it. He gave me those "stop-thinking pills," the same ones most doctors and psychiatrists were prescribing for women with "problems" at that time. I walked out of his office with more Valium than I had ever seen before. What made him so certain I wouldn't down the whole bottle? Of course, he delivered me into the hands of my husband, whose job it was to make certain I took the proper dosage, no less and no more.

This was the woman who, at twenty-two years of age, conceived again as a result of rape. Stoned, tearful, confused and in great pain, she conceived. And her instant reaction to this betrayal from her body (how dare it be fertile? how dare it be female?) was to wish that this fetus too would decide that life was not to be embarked upon at this time and in this place.

The fetus, however, had other ideas, and soon after conception decided it was time to make its presence known to its unwilling host. And this is the dialogue that ensued in my head with the fetus that would become my son. "I want to be born," it said. "I have nothing to give you," I replied. "I want to be born," it said, more emphatically. "I can't care for you, I can't even care about you at this point," I said, weeping now. "I want to be born, give me life." "I can't, I can't," I said; "I don't know how to care for you, won't be able to do it." "Give me life," the fetus said more insistently, "Give me life and the rest will take care of itself. You can give me a great gift — life, that's all I ask." "All? All? What about raising you? I know I won't be able to do it." "Life is the gift I ask," it said again, "Life, life, life …"

We made a bargain, the fetus and I. I would give it life, the only gift I had to offer at that time, with the assurance that this would be enough and that the rest would somehow take care of itself. I didn't know how that could happen. I knew what was expected of me as a mother, but I also knew that it would be okay with this child if all I could do was give it life.

I told this story to my son in his late teens and his immediate reaction was: "You know, Elly, it really is okay." He's not broken in spirit. He's beautiful. It really is okay. What is not okay is what we both missed because I did not have the ability to mother him. And the farther along the path of my healing I travel, the more I realize how much we have missed that is not, ever, recoverable.

❖ ❖ ❖

Once, long ago, there was a time when I did not hate myself. My hating began with my first menstruation. I was not prepared for this event. I thought that I must have been damaged by my father, that the blood was a result of injury. And how was I to present this situation to my mother? Would she be mad at me? What would the punishment be? Why did this happen? When would it stop? And what was I supposed to do with the mess?

I stayed in bed for as long as I could that Saturday morning. I didn't know what else to do, didn't know whom I could tell about this and not suffer terrible consequences. Finally I wadded up a pair of panties and stuffed them inside another pair so I could get out of bed and not make a mess as I walked. But I still didn't know how to tell my mother.

All through that long morning, I tried to find ways to tell her that would not lay the blame for this bizarre bleeding on myself. At the same time, I tormented myself with accusations. I should have stopped him, should never have let (as though I had any choice) him or those other men touch me. I tormented myself with my sinfulness. The bleeding was because I had sinned in some way by not making them stop, or more likely just because I was female and weak. The questions went on and on in confusion, pain and terror. What was I to do? If the bleeding didn't stop, would I die? I saw clearly that this was punishment from God. The fact that I didn't understand what I had done to deserve it didn't change that.

Several times that morning, because I was pale, because I didn't move about the way I usually did, because I tried to sit down every time her back was turned or when she left the room, my mother asked me what was wrong. This only increased my terror. Could she tell? Did it show? A trip to the bathroom proved that there was no blood to be seen on my dress or legs. I sat in the bathroom and wondered what it would be like to die of this bleeding. Would I fade slowly? Would my sisters miss me? Would my mother? Would my father care at all?

The bleeding became a more insistent presence. I would have to tell my mother. I waited for the best time that morning, the time she took her coffee and sat at the table to review what had been done and what was yet to be done to make the house Dutch clean by noon, when my father came home for lunch.

"I want to talk to you about something. Don't tell Dad," I said. "Promise me you won't tell him." "No, I can't promise that. What do you want? Why haven't you finished cleaning the bathroom when you've been in there more than half an hour? What is your problem this morning anyway?" "I don't know what's wrong with me. I'm bleeding, a lot, from down there." She looked at me with that hard look of hers and said, "Oh, is that all? Come with me." She marched me into the bathroom, showed me where the pads were stored, gave me a small elastic belt and showed me how to fasten the pad to it. She told me that I must let no one know what was happening. It was a secret I must learn to keep. I was particularly not to let my brothers or sisters know about this. The pads must be burned in the barrel by the back lane without attracting any attention to what I was doing. "That means you won't tell Dad?" "What?" "If it's a secret, it means you won't tell him." "No, that wasn't what it meant. He'd want to know." "Why?" "Never mind. Get back to work."

"When will it stop?" "It doesn't stop, stupid. It goes on until you're old." "Always? I'll have to wear these things for the rest of my life, always? Why?" "This is what happens to girls. It stops after a few days and then starts again next month." "No," I say, "it can't. I don't want this to be." "Don't be ridiculous," she says. "There's nothing you can do about it. This is the way it is. Quit whining." "Mom, can I go lie down for a while? I don't feel very good." "There's no reason to lie down. Nothing's wrong with you."

"Yes there is, yes there is! I don't want to be a girl if this is what it means. I don't want to bleed every month. It feels terrible; it is terrible. This isn't fair. Does it happen to boys?" "No, all they have to do is shave when they're older." "That's not the same thing. Why do I have to bleed?" "Now you can have babies. When your bleeding starts, it means you can have babies." I am suddenly even more horrified than I was before. Babies? You mean the blood makes babies? Oh no, oh no! Not me, not me ever. I clutch my belly as a cramp begins, bending over in pain. Nausea follows the cramp. Horrible, horrible. Until it stops when I'm an old woman, every month I have to endure this misery? It's not fair, it's not fair.

Fair has nothing to do with it, my mother assures me. It's just the way things are because you're a girl. Then I hate being a girl. This is too terrible. I don't want to be a girl. I don't like anything I have to do because I'm a girl. I want to be a boy. I want to live the kind of life my brother does. Life is easy for him. He doesn't have to clean the house every Saturday. He doesn't have to scrub and wax floors, iron clothes, clean the bathroom or do dishes for twelve people three times a day — and he doesn't have to bleed every month. I hate being a girl. I hate it, I hate it.

Finally I get permission to lie down for a while. And this is when, lying on the couch listening to Saturday morning cleaning rituals going on without me, I first begin to hate myself. I am a prisoner in a body I did not choose. I am a prisoner in a life that becomes more of a nightmare each year, showing me over and over again things I cannot do, or have, or be, simply because I am a girl. Being a girl is the worst thing in the world.

The greater my hatred of my body, the worse my cramps, but I didn't make the connection then. The greater my hatred, the worse my "attitude." No one could come anywhere near me. I snapped and snarled; tried, with a hatred I can barely acknowledge even yet, to scratch my oldest brother's eyes out once. And scared myself so much I finally realized that this course, this expression of my rage, was much too dangerous.

Before the onset of my menstruation each month, I fantasized about killing myself. I could not go on like this, couldn't live with this hateful body, wanted out of it. Oh, how much I wanted out of it! It gave me nothing but pain. First I learned that my father and his friends could do anything they wanted to me. Then I learned that I would bleed every month with pain and discomfort and creepy odours. Was there no end to what this body meant in terms of pain?

I felt that my body had betrayed me, had become an alien thing to which my mind was bizarrely attached. I finally found the courage to ask my mother if there was no other way than old age to stop the bleeding and misery. She told me that it was possible to have an operation to remove the parts that caused the bleeding, but that meant you couldn't have any children, and that it wasn't allowed unless you were very ill. From the moment she told me about the operation, when I was nearly thirteen, it became my goal. I didn't know how I was going to do it, I just knew that at the first opportunity I would have the whole troublesome mess removed from my body. And life would not be able to go forward in the way I dreamt of until that had been taken care of.

I had been dreaming, secretly, of what I would do when I was finally able to leave my father's house. I would be an archaeologist and a writer. I dreamt of travelling to Egypt. I would explore the Valley of the Kings and discover the burial places of the lost queens of Egypt. I would unearth the tomb of Hatshepsut, for I was sure I knew where it was. Hatshepsut, the queen who, when she was told by the priests that she could not rule because she was a woman, had herself proclaimed a man and wore a ceremonial beard strapped to her chin for state occasions. I thought: Hatshepsut never bled. Hatshepsut never had time for this girl nonsense. She knew she was a queen from the moment of her birth and she had the power to banish whatever she didn't like from her life.

How I wished for the power of my heroine queen. Instead, my cycles caused me ever greater pain. Pain that Midol or 222s couldn't touch. Pain that was not only physical, though that was how it made itself known. By the time I was fifteen my mother thought I had better see a doctor. My father gave his permission. He wanted to know if I had been damaged in some way. How? By whom? Never mind, the doctor will check.

The doctor will examine you now. With what terror we hear these words, when they introduce a first visit to the gynecologist. A gruff man in a white coat tells me to take my clothes off and hoist myself up on the examining table. With his foot he pushes a stool toward it so I can climb up, and he tosses me a small sheet with which to cover myself. I'll be back in a few minutes, he says.

It is cold in the little room. The examining table on which I must lie and wait for the doctor looks, with its stirrups, like some torture device, and just like the one my aunt told me she had been strapped to, screaming, during the birth of her daughter. There are strange instruments strewn about on a couple of trays on the window sill. What will he do to me? Why can't my mother be here with me?

The doctor comes back into the room with a stern nurse in tow. He proceeds to the foot of the table and I hear him move things around on the trays. As he does this he tells me to move myself so that my feet are in the stirrups and my ass is exposed. Oh no, not me. I'm not going to do this. I do nothing, pretend I haven't understood him. The nurse comes toward me and informs me that I must cooperate with the doctor, and she places my feet in the stirrups and pushes me toward the edge of the table.

Relax, he says. This isn't going to hurt. What? What? Suddenly he is fumbling about "down there." Oh, oh, what is this, why is he doing this? Take a deep breath, he says, as he shoves something hard, cold and large into me. My whole body contorts in shock and pain. My back arches and I lift myself off the table and try to back away from him. Lie still, he snarls. If you lie still it won't hurt. Some echo in this, surely? Haven't I heard this before? Get away from me, I scream, get away. The nurse is beside me now, telling me not to upset the doctor. The doctor is nearly finished his examination and is telling me to do as I'm told. Echoes, echoes. I realize I'm crying. The doctor has removed whatever it was he put into me, and for now the assault seems to be over. I hear him tell the nurse to "get her dressed and send her mother into my office."

My mother is furious when we meet in the waiting room. I have embarrassed her by being, once again, uncooperative, and by making the doctor upset and angry. Is there something wrong with me then? Do I need the operation? What operation? The one that will stop the bleeding. She looks at me as though a more stupid person has never walked this earth. There's nothing much wrong with you, she tells me, but he's given you a prescription. What's it for? For the pain? No, it's to make you more cooperative. I hope it's worth what it's going to cost.

But the pills do not make me more cooperative. They make me slow, dull, uncaring. I tell her I don't think I need them except just before the bleeding begins. She agrees that my "problems" are worse then, and that the pills can be saved for those times.

❖ ❖ ❖

My mother loved flowers. Of all the things she missed from Holland, what she missed most were the flowers. I remember her sitting at the table on a Saturday morning with a very special kind of coffee she rarely bothered to make for herself, trying to tell me about the flowers in Holland. I had no memories of them and my ten-year-old imagination could not grasp a world so filled with sunshine, colour and scent.

The scent of flowers is still mixed for me with the scent of coffee and floor wax and spring. For only if I worked very fast and very hard and got most of my work done before ten o'clock could we sit together for twenty minutes while she drank her coffee.

I wonder now if she rarely made the special coffee because drinking it always seemed to bring her wave after wave of nostalgia for Holland. I would see this wash over her face and ask her, "What is it, Mom? What are you thinking?" — knowing she was thinking about things far away, things that did not include me, things I wanted, at least then, to hear about. But she told me very little, considering it an indulgence, given that her husband wouldn't like her to tell me much about her past or her childhood.

And these were the only times she sat still with just me. The other kids would be outdoors in spring while we two cleaned the house from the front porch right through to the back step. When I was ten, most of my sisters were still too small to help much, though the sister born just after me would have the care of the little ones. My oldest brother, who was old enough to help, was never required to do anything like housework or dishes.

I didn't mind, then, what work there was to do. The reward was so great: to sit with her, to have her look at me, only me, for just a few precious moments. To hear a little, however little, about her childhood. I remember asking her once who she was before she was my mother. I remember the stunned look on her face as she tried to fathom my question.

The last sip of coffee would mean the end of the magic, and I would be back on my hands and knees scrubbing the bathroom or kitchen floor. As I scrubbed and rinsed, scrubbed and rinsed again to meet her exacting standards, I plotted strategy for the next Saturday, considered other questions I might ask, tried to figure out ways to get her to take a longer coffee break so she would have more time to talk to me.

One spring the talk of flowers and her mother brought such emotion from her that I was surprised — and appalled when I asked her (didn't I realize the import of this until then?) how long it had been since she had seen her mother. Five years? I knew I wouldn't be able to live if I didn't see my mother for five years. She'd just have to go and see my Oma, that was all there was to it. And my mother, my tough, stern, in-control mother, broke down and wept. I can't go, I can't, I can't. Who would look after all you kids and your father? I can't go. There's no money. I can't go.

I knew her parents were not particularly well off, but neither were they poor. So I asked the obvious question: If she had a ticket, if my Oma and Opa (grandfather) lent or gave her the money for a ticket, would she go? She looked startled but interested. And, I said — becoming very excited for her, not realizing what any of it would mean for me, not realizing, not realizing — I could help look after the house and the kids. I do lots of that now.

Reality dawned hard and cold in her eyes as she said: Your father won't let me go. I countered with, tell him you need to, tell him you miss your mother so much that you have to visit her. And tell him you'll feel better and be happier when you get back. And you should write to Oma right now and tell her you need to see her.

I knew that in order for my scheme to get her a visit with her mother to be successful, she would have to write while she still felt strongly about it, before the rest of the many reasons to prevent her leaving us came to the surface, and before she had a chance to tell my father. I fetched her writing case, handed her an aerogram and a pen. Write to Oma now, I said. Tell her how much you miss her and want to see her. I'll bet anything she'll help you with a ticket. I just know she will. And I'll mail the letter before Dad comes home for lunch.

It was urgent that the letter be mailed before he knew about it, and it was also urgent that Oma's reply simply invite her and not refer back to her letter. I told her to make sure she found some way to tell Oma this. I can still see the look on her face as I told her, with this warning, what I really knew about my father. I had learned my lessons well and early, and they were not necessarily what she thought she had taught me. I knew his iron grip on her life. It wasn't any different from his grip on me or on the rest of the household.

I held my breath. Somehow I knew how much she needed to see her mother, to be away from us for a time. All winter she had been desperately unhappy, and when I tried to ask her what was wrong she would not answer me, or would tell me to never mind and get back to work. As I held my breath, I tried to will her the courage to write the letter. The pen came near the paper and stopped. She looked at me. Do it, Mom. Please, please. The pen descended to the paper this time and I watched her begin: *Lieve Moeder*. She stopped again. I waited. And then the words flowed and I knew it would be all right until she got to the end. I went back to my assigned task but kept watch to make sure she continued to write and did not need more encouragement.

Once begun, the letter did not take long to write. She folded it and sat and looked at it. I stood beside her for a few moments, watching the struggle in her face, before I reached out to take the letter. I'll run to the mailbox with it now, I said.

I had expected her reply: I can't send it, your father won't let me send it once he reads it. He doesn't have to see it, I said. I'll mail it right now. You want to see Oma, right? You wrote to her about that, right? Then I'll mail the letter for you. He won't know if you don't tell him, and I won't tell him either. I only wish I could go with you. She handed me the letter and looked at the clock. Run then, she said, and tell the kids you're going to the store for me. Run. He'll be home for lunch in ten minutes.

Every letter from her mother in the month after that excited me. I tried to be near her when she read, so I could watch her face. I questioned her closely. What did Oma say? Can she help? What did Dad say? Can you go? When are you going? Who's going to look after us? Can I go with you? I can't remember now if she went that spring or the one after it. All I know for certain is that she went to Holland for five long weeks, and that it was before my menstrual cycles began.

She almost didn't go. My father did not want to lose her services for so long, didn't know what he'd do without her, didn't think she should waste the money to see her parents when he wanted to spend it on more new toys for himself: camera, stereo equipment, guitar, amplifiers. There was so much he needed, and here she was wasting it to see that stupid old man and her bitch of a mother. I don't know what she said to him finally to get permission to go, but one day he seemed suddenly resigned to the idea, and plans went forward from that time.

A neighbour girl would come in every day to look after us and the house while my father was at work. My father's mother would check in to make sure the hired girl fed him properly. We were to be extra good and not make any trouble for Dad while Mom was away. We were to do as we were told and do it quickly so he wouldn't lose his temper.

There were lists for me: things I had to do for my father because the hired girl could not be trusted to do them. I was instructed how to prepare and when to present his breakfast tea and rusks. I was taught how to properly iron his shirts, press his pants and polish his shoes, and how to lay out all his clothes as soon as he went to the bathroom to shave. I learned how to clean up after him and how to try to stay invisible and out of his way. And I had to move fast in the morning, for everybody had to be dressed and the breakfast porridge had to be made at the same time, so that the older ones could be in school on time and the little ones cleaned up before the hired girl arrived at 8:45.

If my brothers and sisters made too much noise or didn't eat their breakfasts, it was my fault and I would have to pay for it. My father's morning contribution was to yell, shut up, shut up all of you, from the bathroom. And if he was not obeyed instantly, he would storm out, his face contorted and half covered in shaving lather, to threaten us with a beating.

❖ ❖ ❖

I wonder, did my mother ever walk along a Dutch seashore and say what it was she dreamt of doing with her life, to herself or to a friend? And what would it have been like, in her teens during the 1930s, to have dreams as the nightmare of Hitler gathered on the horizon?

Both my mother's and my Oma's generation experienced the devastation of war. Did this influence how they saw the world, how they lived their lives and how they raised their children? What is the relationship between the emotional and physical violence of living in a war zone and the health of the soul even many years after the war is said to have ceased? Does one not carry wounds, great wounds, from such experiences? And if wounds are not properly tended, do they not become greater wounds?

My parents refused to speak about the war. I heard, in all my childhood, only three stories about my father's experiences, and one from my mother, but only in relation to their courting time. My father told me once, as he held me down and forced me yet another time to do what he wanted, that he had used his hands to kill before and that it would be no hardship to do so once again and remove me from the face of the earth. Twice he tried, and these events were pivotal to my understanding of his power to destroy me. Usually all he had to do was bring his hands near my throat for me to comply. I learned that his threats could be carried out, that they were much more than talk, so that every threat he made had the force of fact. It could be done. I could die if I did not learn to obey.

Where and how did he learn to conduct himself in this way? Where did my mother learn that it was better to give in to him, to let him have his way, to comply with his every whim, than to stand her ground and say with the force of her own adult authority that these things would not be done in her house and in her life? Where did my mother acquire such intense loyalty to this man that she was prepared to, and did, sacrifice the health and safety of all her children? Where, and how and why did they learn these lessons? And what, looking at what I know of these lives, can I learn from all of this?

Those of us who tried to grow despite the abuse conducted against us never received the basic respect owed to us as human beings. Our personal integrity, the integrity of our bodies and minds, was violated again and again and again. And while this was done we were lectured about respect by our parents, by our teachers and, on Sundays, by our ministers. And what did we learn? We learned that power is respected, that violence is respected, but that such respect is prompted by fear for the consequences, which, as far as I am concerned, has nothing to do with respect and everything to do with terrorism.

In every context I was threatened. If this or that wasn't done, if I didn't give my father what he wanted, I suffered the miserable and painful consequences. At school, if I didn't do what I was told, I was hauled up before my classmates and strapped across the hands with a thick leather strap. Even among my peers, some would threaten on the playground with the bullying that they had learned from their fathers at home. There was no place I could go where violence against me was not a consideration and a possibility. And if the violence I lived with every day was not enough, in church I was promised that there would be further violence awaiting me the moment life was over.

So what I learned was that there are two kinds of people: those who do and those who are done to. And those who are done to are always the weakest and most vulnerable: children, women, the disabled and the old. And those who do — who neglect, abuse, destroy — are usually men. And I thought it would be far better to side with the doer, for he had power, than to side with the done to, for she did not. As I entered my teens I learned to despise my mother's weakness. And so, to make my destruction complete, I identified with my father and the power I thought he had, by the right I was taught to believe he certainly had, even as he used my child body.

It is a mistake to believe that only my child body was violated. My woman's mind, psyche, soul, were as well, and in many ways. The beginning of healing is to recognize in how many, many ways I have identified with the abusers. Psychologists call it the Stockholm syndrome, when, in order to survive, hostages (and I was a child hostage) identify with their captors. Withdrawing identification with the abuser is much like unravelling a matted and tangled skein of yarn. It takes patience and it takes time — a great deal of patience and even more time.

I grew to adulthood without ever having seen a woman who was strong and healthy and empowered in her own life. So I had no models, and therefore no way to know what goals I might appropriately set for myself. And I thought that, without this identification with power, and the world view that comes with it, there was nothing — or if there was something else, it was bound to be unnatural. Certainly a male-supremacist culture would like me to believe there is nothing else but what they have decided and decreed to be natural for me — which translates into power for them, and victimization for me and everyone else.

The greatest empowerment in my woman's life came when I realized that men and the gods men have constructed in their own image to perpetuate their power and serve their needs are responsible for how I have been defined, and for deciding what is "natural" for me as a woman — and that the men who have done this are very much like the men who abused me, with all their human frailties and fears. And I learned that, as an adult, I need no longer fear them or their gods, the way I had as a terrorized child.

❖ ❖ ❖

I had hoped, that first time my mother went to visit her mother in Holland, that the little yellow rosebush near the lane would be in bloom by the time she returned so that I could give her a bouquet as soon as I saw her. It was too early for the roses or garden flowers, but I remember insisting that my father at least purchase some flowers, even though that meant that they would be from him and would have nothing to do with me.

Weeks later, when the roses in the yard were in bloom, I told her what I had wanted to do on her return. She stunned me by telling me that yellow roses meant treachery and that one must never give yellow roses to a friend. When I asked for an explanation, she said that if a man gave yellow roses to his wife it meant that he had been unfaithful.

I was instantly consumed by a guilt I had not felt until then. He had explained to me that what he asked me to do was something he had been told by my mother I was to do for him. It was not on any of the lists she had made for me before she left, he said, because she had forgotten to include it, but it was something she wanted me to do for him nevertheless. I didn't quite believe him, but he assured

BEYOND DON'T

me that it was part of caring for him and that she would want him properly cared for.

It was reasonable, he assured me. I was the oldest daughter, and just as I was required to take her place in the housekeeping and mothering, I must also take her place in bed. It was my role, the work she had been training me for. I must do whatever he asked of me, so as not to disappoint her and betray her faith that I could handle whatever was necessary while she was away. My mother wanted this, he said finally, but had not known how to ask me.

My mother wanted me to do this. Powerful, powerful words: My mother wanted this. And oh how I missed my mother, and oh how afraid I was that she would never come back! I knew how unhappy she was. And he wasn't sure either that she would come back, though he never said as much. What my mother somehow left off the list of things I was to do was that I was to sleep in their bed, beside him, so that my body was always available to him.

In the beginning he tried to be what he thought of as kind, and said he would teach me what it meant to be a woman and a lover. But I proved untrainable, refused to relax, refused to take part in the ways he demanded. No matter what he tried, my body remained rigid, my thighs clenched, and he satisfied his never-ending hunger by ejaculating against my thighs or back. I soon wore out his patience and the threats began.

When I saw what it meant — to, as I thought, obey my mother in this — I decided that, no matter what it cost me in terms of her anger, I could not obey. But that did not mean I was excused from sleeping with him. I had a duty to perform and it would be done whether I agreed to it or not. My mother was gone for five weeks. Each night, because of my responsibilities for house and children and the comfort of my father — for there was much the hired girl refused or was unable to do — I was the last child to bed. The other children were in their own beds by eight. I was the first one up in the morning, because my father had to have his tea and a buttered rusk as soon as he woke. When the other kids came downstairs, I was already in the kitchen. None of them ever knew where I had spent the night.

His demands exhausted me. I remember asking if we children could not take turns doing these things he continuously assured me he needed. No, he said, my mother's instructions were clear. I was the one she trusted to look after him. I remember bits of his conversation and one or two incidents from this time; most of the rest is a blur. I remember lying on my back and memorizing the pattern in the stained-glass window that I could see from where I lay. I remember thinking how strange it was to take my mother's place. I examined this from every angle, wondering, wondering, wondering how my mother could live like this with him.

I remember trying to make myself into someone else, someone from the fairy tales I read with such compulsion at that time. I was both the child who was lost and needed rescue and the one who did the rescuing. I rode a beautiful horse across a land of beauty and wonder. I was a princess with enough wealth and power to demand that other girls take my place in my parents' bed. I was someone else, always, torn between doing what my mother wanted and my sense that, if this was what she wanted, there was no way at all for me to live in my body.

I remember conversations with him. Remember how loath he was to touch his own genitals, and how curious and insistent he was about touching mine. My stubborn refusal to relax and accept my responsibility and fate as girl eventually resulted in different tactics, and he demanded that I use my mouth on his penis. And here too I could not do adequately what he wanted, and from this began the notion that I was stupid. Too stupid for words. Stupid, stupid, so stupid I could not follow the simplest of instructions.

My mother returned to an excited and joyful welcome. I hoped that as soon as she saw me she would acknowledge what I had done for her all those weeks, and I hoped that she would do this with a gift and would thank me. For if these things were done by my mother, the nagging sense I had that what had happened would not be all right with her would leave me. And perhaps it would be possible then to tell her that it had been too difficult a task for me and to complain about his treatment of me.

In my turn I stood in front of her to greet her, and waited. She said nothing. Perhaps she had forgotten? Well, she said finally, were you good while I was gone? Yes, I said. I did everything you told me to. And I was so good that I only needed one spanking, but it will last me the rest of my life. She looked from me to my father and he said, "I'll tell you later." And I was nudged from my place in line and the next child said hello. Only the very small kids got anything like a hug. I got a frown, a severe look and dismissal, nothing like the thanks or acknowledgement I wanted so much.

To say I was disappointed would be a gross understatement. I was devastated. How could she not know what it had cost me to do all the things she had left for me to do? How could she dismiss me like that? How could she be so cruel? As I walked away I folded in on myself, holding onto tears until I was well out of her sight. Behind me I could hear the conversations she had with my brothers and sisters, and these seemed to me to be filled with warmth and interest. For me there had not even been that. And I had been dismissed, there was no mistaking that, while the others could hover round her with their chatter, and that was fine with her.

A spanking to last my whole life was what I had said. And she had not asked what it was for, let alone why I described it that way. "Spanking" was the word he had used for the beating he gave me, a beating he applied with his hands and a wicker rug beater. A beating so severe that I passed out and had to be shaken awake so that I could be sent to bed. A beating so severe it left welts on my lower back and buttocks, some of which bled enough to make my night-dress stick to them. A beating so severe I was in bed for three days, unable to move.

I remember that my father's mother arrived on the third day to demand why I was pretending to be sick. Before she came upstairs, he had been up to see me and tell me that, if I told her what he had done, he would finish what he had started and kill me. He need not have worried. I neither liked nor trusted his mother and would have told her nothing. She demanded that I stop my laziness and get back to work; didn't ask me what was wrong; assumed that, as I was my mother's daughter, I was lazy.

I knew his mother's opinion of my mother. She made no secret of what she considered to be my mother's physical flaws and personal as well as housekeeping defects. I vacuumed her rugs every Saturday. I knew what she thought of my ability to do a thing right: non-existent. And here I was, just as she'd always thought I would be some day, hiding out in bed instead of working — my mother's daughter to be sure.

I wonder how anyone, ever, can make accusations of laziness against a woman (or her helper daughter), who keeps a spotless house and whose eight, nine, then ten scrubbed kids show up in church every Sunday morning in neatly ironed clothes and polished shoes. And I wonder why.

His mother was dissatisfied with the interview she had with me. I heard her downstairs telling my father that she had given me a talking to and that there was nothing wrong with me. But she could not tell him when I would get up, for I persisted in saying I was too sick to move, even though she thought I didn't look a bit sick.

And this is how I was trained to be a slave, putting my father's interests before my own, always. For as a slave I had no legitimate interests to see to or protect. And I had no power. This is how I learned to lie to save face for a master, first for my father and later for the other men I had contact or relationships with. Saving their reputations became more important than saving my life.

What I should have done, I see now, was show her my back and scream and carry on about what he'd done to me. Instead I protected him — partly because I believed I had somehow deserved it (even if I could not figure out precisely what I had done) and was ashamed, and partly because I knew that, if I did show her and complain, he would beat me again, and I truly did not know if I would survive a second beating that severe.

❖ ❖ ❖

My father did not believe that my mother should get what she needed, or what she wanted. That privilege he reserved for himself. Nor was she entitled to keep what she brought from Holland. At least, this is the conclusion I draw from years of watching him destroy everything her mother had given her for her home. If my mother was to have anything, it had to be something like a dress so that she could display her body in a way he called sexy. The ornaments and figurines she enjoyed so much because they came from Holland, or reminded her of Holland and her mother, he destroyed, every one.

I remember thinking that the little bronze lizard, one of the last pieces to survive, would make it because it would not break if dropped. I thought the lizard ugly, but dusted it with care each week because it was one of the few things left from Holland for my mother to love. The other figurines fell to pieces when he moved the furniture without taking care to move them to safety, or when he placed something too near them, and knocked them over the edge of the table. The little lizard survived many trips to the floor without so much as an extra dent in its surface, until the day he had to make some adjustment to the back of the television. He reached for the little lizard and used its body as a hammer, and in doing so snapped off the tail. I think my mother was beyond tears by this point, for she did not react at all.

In the household where I grew up, only my father got to buy things he wanted. It didn't matter what it cost the rest of us for him to spend our resources on rye whisky to entertain his friends, or to buy a camera rather than pay the grocery bill. If we didn't eat, that was just "too goddamn bad."

The summer I was fifteen I got a job in a local drugstore and was paid ninety-five cents an hour. I worked from twenty to thirty-five hours a week. At the end of the week I was to give my unopened pay packet to my father. Out of my earnings he would hand me five dollars, and pocket the rest.

Once I was launched with my own job, he no longer felt it necessary to contribute to my maintenance in any way. If I wanted clothes, shoes or underwear, I had to save my five dollars a week and purchase them myself. If I wanted to take the bus to and from work rather than walk, I had to take that out of my five dollars. If I wanted to eat a plate of fries before nine-thirty at night, when I got home to a dinner that had been kept warm in a bowl in the oven since five-thirty, that too had to come out of my five dollars. If I wanted butter on my bread, as he had, rather than the margarine the children got, I had to pay him a dollar a week for the privilege.

And when, two years later, I quit school, depressed beyond belief because I was convinced he had the power he claimed to make sure I never got to university, and began a full-time job with a salary of $160 a month, I got $40 and he got the rest. No amount of begging could change this, and I certainly did beg him to be more generous. For I was by then saving, or trying to save, enough money to buy the things I needed to leave home.

Who tells me that I may not have what I want, and why? Who tells me that if I have the money and buy what I need, I will be punished? Who tells me I may not spend whatever money I earn in whatever way I please? Who tells me that if I spend this little bit of money my way, I will never get any more? Who tells me that if I spend my money now, I will starve next year? Who tells me, and why?

I begin to see something of why I twist myself so out of shape about money. Even yet, my own money makes me uncomfortable, as though I have to spend it before he? — someone? — finds out and takes it from me. Buying something I need for the kitchen seems a gross waste of my resources. Buying clothes, even on sale, results in terror that I am spending grocery money foolishly, when this is certainly not the case. This year, at least, I have more than five dollars a week.

❖ ❖ ❖

The list of things stolen from me seems endless. And now I have come to a place at the core of my sense of my writer self. My first language was not English. In nursery school in Holland, when it became known that I would go to Canada, we all began to learn words and phrases in English. I loved English the way a child loves a secret language she speaks to her dolls.

It was exhilarating to learn the way things were described in another language, that *fleighteug* was a "plane," that *dank u wel* became "thanks a lot," that Oma became "Grandmother," and that when asking for something in Canada I would have to remember to always say "please, may I" before making my request. My schoolmates and I were all highly amused by the strange sounds we made trying to say things in acceptable English.

I practised and practised. It was such fun. Though I did not want to leave Holland and my Oma, I was excited about the idea of being in a place where I would get to try out my English. I suggested to my mother that I would like to visit just long enough to speak English for a little while, and then I wanted to come home.

On the train from Montreal I was finally brave enough to attempt English. I asked a conductor for something, once, twice, three times. He appeared not to hear me. And it dawned on me that I must not be saying it correctly, for he did not understand what I wanted. I was so disappointed. What could be wrong? I didn't have any sense that I had a thick Dutch accent on my English phrase. All I knew was that I had practised so hard I must be saying the right words.

It did not take long for me to begin to miss the sound of Dutch around me. It is difficult to suddenly have to live your life in another language. Initially you understand so little. You become more and more certain that you aren't understanding things the way they are meant. It is embarrassing to ask for an explanation for every phrase or euphemism. And you take everything literally, and have the neighbour kids hooting with laughter at your stupidity. So you stop trying to understand and only pretend that you do, that you always know exactly what is meant, even though you're still in the dark.

At school it was worse. There were rules and there were interpretations of rules. If I missed the sense of something, I was in trouble. So I learned to do nothing unless I saw someone else do it first and win approval. I learned to keep my mouth shut because only the wrong words seemed to come out when it was open. I pretended stupidity when I was merely afraid of making a fool of myself and being laughed at.

The language of my childhood, the language I shared with my mother and grandmother, was no longer mine by the time I was eight. My mother still spoke Dutch to my father, but he had made it clear that he did not want her to speak Dutch with us, for we were to be Canadian now. The nuns punished me for speaking Dutch to my sister in class and then separated us so we were no longer in the same room. I was told that I was not allowed to speak Dutch on the school grounds, not even to my sister, not even at recess.

I rarely heard Dutch spoken and there were no Dutch books to read. I tried sometimes to make lists of the Dutch words I knew, but I'd never learned to spell them and I found I had no vocabulary at all, could not write words like "sister," "house," "school," "teacher," and I did not know enough words to write letters to my Oma. Even my accent, which I learned to cherish as a reminder of who I was, faded from my speech.

I had lost my ability to speak in my own voice. It had disappeared somewhere between having to lie about what was happening to me and the loss of my Dutch. English became, for me, the language of lies. This has many interesting reverberations in my life as a writer since it makes me so wary of my own words that the writing process is much slower than it needs to be. When I visited my grandmother in Holland on the book tour for *Don't*, the first thing she said to me was: "Where's your Dutch, girl?" Where indeed?

I transferred my allegiance to English when I realized that it was possible to read books in English. I decided that I would now sing "God Save the Queen" and mean their queen, not the one I considered mine because she was the Dutch queen. I thought about this carefully for many weeks before deciding that, because I did not even have a picture of the Dutch queen in my mind any more, and there were beautiful pictures of Queen Elizabeth II available, it would make more sense to pray for and sing the song for someone I could imagine, and even see in the official portrait that hung in the school.

I tried to discuss with my mother what, for me, was an important issue: whether I should give up being Dutch and wishing good health for the Dutch queen, and become English (not Canadian, never Canadian) and sing for the English queen. My mother did not seem to understand how important my decision was. She assured me that — no matter that I no longer felt Dutch or spoke the language — I was still Dutch because I had been born in Holland.

For the next twenty-five years I did not know who I was, or even, for much of that time, who I wanted to be. I was stranded between languages and countries, unhappy here and surer all the time that the country I had left behind would not be home either. Where was I to find a home and a place in which I could finally be myself? And was I Dutch? Canadian? Something else entirely?

As an adult and a writer, I experience the loss of my first language, my mother tongue, as a trauma in the order of a major amputation. Some part of me is gone, I think, forever. Only the hunger, a distant echo of it once having been there, remains. For it is not only the language, the words, that seems closed to me; it is the culture, an understanding of my mother's and grandmother's worlds.

I grew up bereft of a language and culture that I loved and needed, and then was required to somehow fit into a language and culture that had no place for me — an immigrant, a foreigner, a woman. I was thousands of miles from the one culture, and, though I lived surrounded by the other, there was no way I was allowed in.

To say I was lonely, lost and confused barely describes how I felt. I thought that the reason I did not fit into Canadian culture was that so much of my Dutch self, though I could not see or feel it any more, was still vitally present. What I finally realized was that my original language and culture were not nearly as problematic as my gender. As a woman, I am always a foreigner in, and never a citizen of, the patriarchal country. It would not have been any different had I remained in Holland.

❖ ❖ ❖

The destruction of my being, sense of self, personal integrity, and connections to my mother and grandmother made relentless progress, so that by the time I was eighteen I was without any sense of self; a shadow in my own life, without feeling, without energy, without hope. The young woman who left home at eighteen had nothing with her when she left. She was a husk.

The woman who found an abandoned church to crawl into when she was twenty-seven was not much different from the eighteen-year-old who had left her father's house hand in hand with her new husband, except that her pain had increased so much that she was forced to do something, anything, to change her life.

Suicide was always an option. For more than ten years I kept enough pills on hand to kill myself. My emergency supply, I called it — the emergency being when I could tolerate the pain no more, the pain that everyone told me I did not have. To get pills I had to be sick. And all my pain was focused on my menstrual cycle. If I did not have these things, a womb, ovaries, if I were not a woman, if I did not bleed, if I did not have hanging over me the sentence of pregnancy and a child to care for, I thought, then I would have a chance in the world. I would be able to do something other than feel so trapped and afraid.

One of the things we do as abused children and adults is slash and hurt ourselves. The extent varies, from scratches to suicide. I did not technically slash myself; I went to doctors and asked them to do it. I found a way to slash myself and keep my denial intact, for the operations, all of them, were legitimate, things I needed to help me get well. The first one was abdominal surgery to tie my tubes. The second was to repair damage done in the first operation and to do a partial hysterectomy. The third was to remove a tumour that had attached itself to the remaining ovary. The first was at twenty-six, the second at thirty and the third at thirty-nine. Each surgery was through the abdomen, with an incision from navel to pubic bone. Each, I think now, was an attempt on my part to remove anything that related to my woman self. If my reproductive system could be excised, I would not have to be a woman, have a woman's life, be sentenced to what my father and society assured me would be my fate — living chained to a man, doing what I was ordered by him to do.

Each surgery made me inordinately happy. I rejoiced in the tiny hope that now I could do something with my life. Now I would not have to worry about pregnancy, deal with a body that always betrayed me in some new way through my reproductive system. What a bizarre concept, betrayal by my own body. How can a body betray itself? Perhaps in this sense: I did not want to be what my father assured me was all I could be — a vessel (more like a toilet than I like to think) for men. The difference between being a girl and being a woman was that, as a girl, I had less control over which men used me. What was constant, not negotiable, ordained for always, natural, was that I would be used because I was a woman.

No, I did not ever wish that I had a penis instead. That's another one of those male egocentricities that men have sanctified as theory. I simply did not want to be used. If my body meant that I was to be used, and have no life apart from being used, then my body had betrayed me, and it made sense that I should remove the parts that men used me for. My sense was that men wanted to use me to get children out of me, and then trap me into caring, alone and without resources, for whatever children I produced.

Each month I fought the war with my body: against use; against the possibility of reproduction; against the reminders, reminders that it made so obvious and with such pain that I was a woman, one of the done to and used; and against the creeping awareness that something in my life was desperately wrong. Denial was so much harder to hang onto during the time of my menstruation. I never understood, then, why.

I must have made hundreds of visits to various doctors, until I found one who would do a hysterectomy. It was a search I began not long after my son was born. The tubal ligation still left a fraction of a chance of pregnancy, at least in my mind, and menstruation after it was even more pain-filled than before.

❖ ❖ ❖

I look at this life and wonder what it all means. Wonder why this had to be my life, why I could not have what I wanted. My mother told me when I was small that people never got what they wanted and that no exception would be made by life for me. I think now that this must have been what she was told, and her mother before her. I don't believe for a minute that men with power don't get what they want, but there is a cost they have never acknowledged or counted. Just as there is a cost and constant hunger born of not getting what you need and want, there is, I think, a great cost to those who take more than their share.

I believe the planet has more than enough resources to nourish all of us. All of us. And I further believe that, if some of us do not have what we need and others have more than they can ever use, it is the greed of those with too much that keeps the rest of us from having enough. And this works on the level of household economy, where my father had more food and protein than he could eat and the rest of us went hungry, as well as on a more global level, where colonial powers have monopolized resources and have created systems in which a few white males have had the power to keep women and children and people of colour from having enough to feed themselves; or from having proper housing and clothing. So if the injustice of my father's house offends, how much greater is the offence of a system that reproduces this same life, with variations, for millions of women, children and minorities the world over?

But it is much easier to demand that my father and others like him be punished than it is to demand the end of the system that allows and encourages abusers of power. Much easier to single out one individual for punishment than to demand that those with power be accountable for the way they treat children, women and the planet. I believe my father is not some aberration of the ideology called patriarchy. He is doing just what he always knew he was entitled by it to do. And this is what causes me despair. Nothing done to my father, no punishment he received, would change my life. Nothing he could be made to suffer, by any prosecution or punishment, would return my childhood to me and give me a healthier one. And yes, I think he ought to be accountable for what he did. But exactly what form would this accountability take, and what compensation could ever be enough?

One of the things it took me the longest to understand was that my father's behaviour was not unusual. By late in my thirties I realized that the statistics I read meant there were many, many other women and men who had been beaten and sexually assaulted as children. But statistics do not have faces. It was only when I began to meet the women and men behind the statistics that the realization really connected. An abused child such as I was is taught to be a selfless slave whose sole purpose is to serve the interests of the master, even at the cost of her or his life. I see the results of this abuse of power in myself and in many other adults I have met who are struggling with their pasts.

I recognize the residual effects of this violence against me in the many ways I continued to serve my father's interests even after writing *Don't*. I almost burned the manuscript when it came back from the publisher for minor revisions — not, as one might think, to protect myself, but to protect my father and the other men it described. And this is one of the things I thought: What if I'm wrong? What if I have misremembered it all? Knowing full well that I only wished my memories to be inaccurate. And another thing I thought was that I now had a responsibility to protect my mother. But the main reason I wanted to destroy the manuscript was because I was still afraid of what my father would do to me once I told. This was how I was enslaved, cowering still as an eleven-year-old before his viciousness, even though I was then forty.

The fact that I could not tell my story and be heard as a child is understandable, though certainly not acceptable. The fact that as an adult I still find the lessons I learned as a child reverberating so strongly in my life horrifies me. For this is how child abuse continues to exist; by not telling our stories when it is finally safe to do so, we allow child abuse to continue in our families and in our communities. Silence literally kills. It kills us first, and goes on to destroy those around us. Our silence protects, not ourselves, but the abusers.

I dream of a time when every woman will have a healthy enough sense of her self and her safety that she can tell her story. Not all abuse looks like mine. There are many, many ways to abuse and destroy a child, each method vicious and all equally devastating. We are so fragile as children, so in need of care and nurturance; it takes so little to harm us.

Dreaming Past the Dark

I wonder if the world is any different today for a child at risk of abuse than it was ten or thirty or fifty years ago. And if it is, what exactly is this difference? And if, as I suspect, very little has changed for children in abusive situations, why?

In the 1970s, the first books were published that documented the horror and extent of the abuse of children. Between the mid-1960s and late 1980s, the incidence of child sexual abuse went from an estimated 1 in 100,000 to 1 in 1,000, to 1 in 4. By the end of the 1980s, hundreds of books on the subject of child sexual abuse had been published. The authors of many of these books did the television talk-show and radio open-line-show circuits — and were promptly co-opted as entertainment.

Entertainment was never the goal when these books were written. Change was the goal, real change: protection and rights for children; changes in political will to ensure that we find, and implement, effective deterrents and treatment for abusers, that we find a way to compensate those who have endured the gross torture that is child abuse and that we stop abuse — now.

I am becoming increasingly concerned about those many children, women and men who have survived abuse in childhood only to be further abused by the prevailing notions of what this means. Current efforts to have abuse taken seriously appear to have generated a cult of victimhood, instead of a societal will to change; those who suffer are absorbed into a system whose interests are served at the expense of, and are deemed to be much more important than, the rights and needs of the abused.

The focus of the media has nearly always been the same: the victim and plenty of details about how she or he was victimized. During most of the television and radio interviews I did for *Don't*, I was never described as anything other than a victim. I was not an author with a political agenda, not a survivor of child abuse committed by a group of men, but always, relentlessly, a victim. And what was done to "victimize" me was of much greater interest than who the perpetrators were. The perpetrators were erased, made invisible. How very convenient for them!

I tried to make the point that I am a survivor; that, if I were still a victim, I would not be in that studio, giving that particular interview. It didn't matter, though. In the next breath I would be called a victim once again. The fact that I had survived to tell about my childhood appeared to be of no interest whatsoever. The fact that I had written a book was rarely discussed and apparently had no importance in these contexts. Some truly enlightened media types appeared to think I had vomited the book, so perhaps that was what was behind their unwillingness to call me the author of it.

What does it mean when a society and the media that represent it are willing to parade the pain of women and children across the television screens of a nation, but are not willing to do anything that in any way points out that there are abusers and an entire system of privilege that supports those who abuse and absolves them of guilt and responsibility for what they do? Why do we not have television talk shows *ad nauseam* where the abusers are required to explain what they did to the children, where they got their ideas from, how they felt about what they did and why they enjoyed it? Why do we not make a circus of *their* lives?

But, you see, it doesn't make for good entertainment to zoom in on a bunch of ordinary male citizens accused by their children of being abusers. Child abuse is a crime in which only the victims have entertainment value, and there are big bucks and great ratings in celebrating all the different ways women and children can be abused, humiliated and tortured.

As long as the issue of child abuse is made into a freak show on the talk shows every afternoon, any call for change, however passionate — and eventually any reporting of abuse, however horrible — will be effectively silenced, slotted, as it is, in between advertisements for new tampons, hair colour and the latest super-clean, non-polluting, biodegradable detergent. The abuse of children will not stop, or even become slightly less prevalent, but it will be nicely swept back under the carpet as the media go on with their cultural mandate to manipulate the next issue.

I once thought, naïvely it turns out, that the reason nothing was being done to protect children or deal in anything like an appropriate way with abusers was that people didn't know the abuse was happening. If people knew what sort of things went on, I thought, they would be stopped. I believed the rhetoric I had heard about how valued children were and how deserving of protection. Yet in my travels to promote *Don't* I found not only that people did know about this issue, but that an amazing number of them had experienced abuse and were now dealing not only with their own painfully remembered abuse, but also with the stories they were beginning to hear from their own children. We were not talking about abuse much in the early 1980s, but it seems everybody knew about it — from experience.

I now see that I and numerous colleagues over the years have been breaking the silence over and over again, only to have it subsequently swallow us up again moments after we speak. The abuse of children, especially of girls, remains normal, invisible and silenced. The media report only those sensational cases where large numbers of child victims are involved. Why? Do we as a society really not give a damn about kids? Do we cherish children only as some idealized image, status symbol, fashion accessory? What could possibly explain the contempt and abuse children so often receive instead of the nurturing and respect they need and deserve?

The simple answer is that people replicate what they know. In the words of one of my sisters, as she slapped her six-month-old baby with a wooden spoon, "If it was good enough for me, it's good enough for my kid. That's how I learned" — an argument that says that, if you were abused or starved or tortured, the only way to feel better is to do exactly the same thing the first chance you get. We need to take revenge? On children? Whose agenda is this?

The more complex answer is that, to a degree I wish I didn't have to see, children share the low status and value still accorded to women, while they have the added problem of not being old enough to leave an abusive situation, have their stories believed or, most important, vote.

In the past, abuse was rarely disclosed. Now that disclosures are made and more often believed, and women try to take action to protect and support their children, I wonder how much children and mothers benefit from current societal responses.

There are now for-profit therapies that cost more than I or most other women earn in a year. At a recent conference on child abuse, I saw an eighteen-metre row of tables groaning under the weight of self-help books on aspects of abuse I had never imagined. Child sexual abuse has gone from being an issue on which every magazine, newspaper and television program does a special, to being an issue that fuels a proliferation of books and psychological services that many who suffer from abuse simply cannot afford.

Too often, despite the mother's active campaign, the child gets minimal, if any, help or therapy, often because the mother cannot afford to pay, or because programmes have been cancelled after the funds for them have been cut. Symptoms of the child's distress are papered over with drugs like Ritalin. Ritalin may be better than nothing, but it isn't a solution, merely a postponement of the problem. Real help in the form of extensive and appropriate therap~

is costly, while Ritalin is cheap. I fear for the children who are given such drugs instead of help toward healing their wounds.

In Canada, the public was for a while (six months, a year?) willing to listen to stories about abuse of children and give a collective "tut, tut, isn't that terrible" response. For a time it seemed to me there would be real movement in all aspects of dealing with the abuse against children. I heard of an occasional aggressive prosecution of perpetrators, though too rarely did I hear of even well-prepared cases succeeding. The most appalling example of injustice I heard was the story of a thirteen-year-old girl. The father was convicted and given a three-month sentence for abusing his daughter. Upon his release from prison, he applied for custody of his daughter and it was granted.

Today, only dramatic cases with multiple victims make much headway in the courts. One or two children accusing a father, stepfather or mother's boyfriend have considerably less success in getting serious attention from the justice system, less chance of conviction, and still less of adequate sentencing should there be a conviction. Too little is known about the proper questioning of children once allegations are brought forward; too few social workers, police, lawyers, crown prosecutors and judges have specialized training in the field of child-abuse prosecutions.

One reason for cases foundering in the courts is that groups promoting the concept of false memory syndrome publicly call into question the credibility of the victims, and defence lawyers call members of such groups as "expert witnesses." The result of the actions of these organizations, which appear to be dedicated to destroying the credibility of children and survivors, is to make us doubt ourselves. For if we doubt ourselves, we will not fight back. I consider the existence of these groups a predictable reaction to bringing these cases to court, for their adherents often include individuals who have been accused of the sexual abuse of children but who, for various reasons, were not convicted. It is the messages these groups are giving to the world that make me uneasy. What am I to make of statements such as this from a recent group newsletter: "We are a good looking bunch of people: greying hair, well dressed, healthy, smiling ..." Is this supposed to mean that nice guys with grey hair and big smiles don't rape children? This certainly has not been my experience.

Apart from the lack of headway in the courts, it is difficult not to be overwhelmed by cynicism in the face of devastating cuts to welfare and social programmes, many of which impact primarily on women and children. Without the support of welfare, interim shelter in transition houses and numerous other social programmes, women often cannot leave abusive husbands. And what becomes of the children then? It is as though society is ever willing to absorb the fact that thousands of children are being or have been abused, but unwilling to allocate sufficient resources to stop the abuse, to provide appropriate services to victims or to make restitution. What we have is plenty of rhetoric about the horror of it all, and nothing much in the way of cash for programmes or protection.

Rebuilding a life that has been devastated by child abuse is, as I hope is generally now known, no easy task. It is an even more difficult task to imagine rebuilding a society where vast numbers of the citizens have suffered severe and debilitating trauma as children. Perhaps things are changing — I'm not convinced yet — but if they are, they are changing much too slowly. There are ever more child victims, and ever more adult survivors who finally feel strong and safe enough to remember what was done to them when they were small.

The long healing process I went through prior to writing *Don't* demanded that I devote enormous amounts of quiet time to it: time without the demands of relationship, job, family and all the other things I expected for myself. The patriarchal society in which we live isn't structured around long sabbaticals during which people can retire to work out their personal difficulties. I think that since child abuse is the product of this same patriarchal society, we are entitled to find our healing path as we choose. What society demands instead is that we get quick fixes through instant-recovery programmes lasting three months or less. The healing work we must do, however, requires time out, and the length of time varies from person to person. What we are told then is that we are lazy, and that welfare won't support or encourage us in this folly we call healing work.

Children's rights, well-being and protection, and all the resources needed to achieve and maintain them, must be on every political agenda. We must find a way to protect children and women from violence. No society that preys on its young has any chance of survival. A society that does not commit adequate resources to stopping violence and to healing the wounds cannot expect to be healthy, productive or successful in any way that counts. If we continue our short-sighted patchwork approach to dealing with child abuse and violence against women, it will wind up costing all of us in ways we haven't even learned to measure yet.

I've been giving a lot of thought to this state of affairs. I've been asking that age-old, discomfiting question: Why? Why as a society do we deem it important to study issues, but not important to provide the financial and human resources to deliver services that make a difference to the lives of women and children? It's not that we don't know what needs doing. It's not that we don't have willing, trained, committed people to do the work. It's something else. But what?

Somehow the entire dialogue around child sexual abuse has stayed focused on individual horror stories, on the problems of individuals and how well they do or do not cope. But society as a whole denies there is a problem, even as this problem is studied to death. Victims are the problem; victims are studied. Isn't something missing here?

As long as people who struggle with everything from stresses caused by poverty and unemployment to the residuals of a childhood like mine are busy just trying to get through today, they are not demanding that the society in which they live in effect changes that will make it possible for them to live full and healthy lives. A destabilized population, where trauma-induced illness is rife, is easy to gouge, to govern and to oppress. Of course, such a population requires occasional mopping up, but there's a vast and growing infrastructure of volunteer organizations that can keep things from getting too far out of hand.

The escalating body count will continue as long as society as a whole maintains the following denial-based illusions: that child abuse is the individual problem and responsibility of the victim rather than a social problem requiring political will and extensive public resources to resolve it; that the nuclear family as currently constructed is a safe place rather than a threatened primary social unit that could be improved by a rethinking, and perhaps restructuring, to ensure that it functions as a nurturing environment for children; that children are the sole responsibility of one or possibly two adults rather than the responsibility of all members of a healthy community; that there is no effective treatment for abusers and no possible deterrent, when what is really at issue is the lack of resources to fund programs and seek solutions; and, finally, that everything will be fine as long as we can find a way to process a few of the most adversely affected victims by applying what I can see only as Band-Aids, such as inadequate short-term therapies, followed by injunctions to the victims that they simply get over it. This is denial at its most pervasive and dangerous.

I don't think I'd get much argument about the statement that healthy people make a healthy community. But do we really want healthy communities? If we consider the social ill represented by the abuse of children, we don't have to search far for its cause. We know that more than 95 percent of abuse is perpetrated by men; that these men feel they have some sort of inherent right to do the vilest things to children or women; and that they need not fear punishment unless they get carried away and kill. The rule of law, which we supposedly live with in a democracy, implies redress for wrongs and compensation for hurt and harm, yet this rule does not apply consistently and significantly to the crime of child abuse. Why are we so unwilling to look at what this means?

Child abuse is a shell game played with the victim. The victim is a shill, a decoy, to keep our attention off the perpetrator and the deeper issue of child abuse in society. The victim is the person we hear about in the media, and things are fine as long as the story is kept at this level. If the victim tries to effect change in the status quo, however — say, by taking her story into a court of law and making allegations against the abuser — nine times out of ten the fact that she has been abused is deemed to make her allegations suspect. Is this justice? Or is it, rather, gender politics? Now we see the crime, now we don't.

If the focus is kept on the victims, we are not thinking about who abuses and why. If we talk about dysfunctional families or family violence — which is the other side of this coin — there are victims and families but never abusers. And "dysfunctional" is such an all-encompassing term that it is being applied equally to families in distress over poverty and those in which children are raped. While there is no doubt that poverty is wretched, it is not the same thing as incest. The concept of dysfunction is neutral and has no political charge. Child abuse, seen through a feminist analysis, has a potent political charge, and that has now been all but silenced in the mainstream media. This feminist analysis describes power relations, and child abuse is about power over children and the adults they grow up to be.

Why is there such resistance to naming the abusers? And just who benefits from a myopic focus on the victim, whether as a statistic or as entertainment? Not the children and not the thousands of adults who are haunted and crippled by what they endured as children. It is the prevailing distribution of power and privilege of a patriarchal society that benefits — and it benefits mightily.

How else are we to understand the fact that, although there have been two major federal studies in Canada in less than ten years, and hundreds of smaller studies and needs-assessment surveys, we still do not have anything like major financial resources dedicated to the issue of child abuse — for children, adult survivors or perpetrators? Yes, I know there are programmes and thousands of caring individuals, many of them volunteers, who give generously of their time and energy. There are hundreds of organizations doing their absolute best and more. But every single programme in the country is under-funded and struggling daily with increasing demands for services.

Power over children, and the right to do to them whatever one wants, is the very basis, cornerstone and underpinning of our social structure, especially within the apparently sacrosanct nuclear family.

If children have rights — and some people acknowledge that they do — these rights, even those defined by the United Nations Convention on the Rights of the Child, are not considered if they challenge adult rights, whether in society generally, in the home or, especially it seems, in the courts. The rights of the most heinous perpetrator are weighed and protected before the right of a child to safety and health. To do otherwise, it is claimed, would subvert the entire judicial system — a statement then used to justify doing nothing or little to address the needs and rights of children.

As a child who was abused, I experienced life as a war zone. I knew as a girl that war was being made against me, against my body, against my budding sense of who I was or might become, against my being, because I was young, female, vulnerable and unprotected. No war is waged if the would-be conqueror believes there is a danger of defeat. War is waged because the victory is assumed to be easy. And it is very easy in today's society to conduct war against children. The atrocities committed are not only sexual assault. There are many other tortures inflicted on young bodies, minds and souls. And what do you have as a society, what product do you have, in the child who has been abused and assaulted all through her or his growing years? Do you have a strong, healthy, capable young person ready to take on life's tasks with commitment and joy? Hardly.

Children who grow to maturity in a war zone, what are they like? Are they happy, healthy, contented, sure of themselves, pretty much like other children deemed not to have grown up in a war zone? Or are they anxious, fractured in spirit, destroyed in body and mind, living lives of barely concealed terror? How does the happy girl child conduct herself? And what behaviour do we see in the damaged girl child?

What is too often found is a cowering slave so afraid of her own shadow that she won't go out of doors, so afraid of life that she will do nothing to engage with it but instead follows the narrow track patriarchy has always decreed as "natural" and God-ordained for her: silent, obedient, demanding nothing. For example, the residual effects of abuse in my life mean that for thirty years the energy required to realize my potential as a writer and artist was entirely absorbed by the need to cope with the effects of my childhood. Worse, an abused child learns, as an adult, to abuse herself. This is not an accident that happens to a few of us by some bizarre twist of fate.

I hear your incredulity: Oh, come on, you say. People are no longer enslaved. Women's lives are pretty good, all in all. Look how far we've come. Yes, and we can own property now, and we can keep the wages we make from our jobs (at least we have a legal right to do so), and we make almost 70 percent of what men make. Yes, right, that's pretty good, I suppose, considering where we were a mere hundred years ago.

Children who grow up with respect of their persons, with love for who they are, grow into strong and healthy young people. Children who have resources, from food to housing to education and beyond, are less likely to grow up to destroy themselves, each other or the planet. I believe that if you respect a child, that child will respect you in turn. I believe that you teach children respect for themselves and others — and that includes all other life forms, and the planet — by, first and foremost, respecting them. And I believe that adults must earn the respect of children.

If all of us truly cared about the health of children and the planet they will one day inherit, we would change how society treats children. We would build daycare spaces with one worker for every three children, or creches at workplaces so mothers and fathers could care for children. Maternal or paternal leaves would be as long as necessary for both the child and the parent. Abused children would get instant attention and access to a long-term (lifelong, if necessary) programme designed to meet their needs in the healing process. We would put our society's resources first into caring for and educating children, and then into everything else.

Yet even if tomorrow we had programmes for all the children, women and men who, against great odds, have been able to speak of the abuse they endured, it would not be enough. For as long as the focus is only on bandaging the seriously wounded, we will always have greater numbers of damaged than we have resources to help them. It isn't difficult to see that the abuse must be stopped at the source, must never take place in any child's life. It's obvious enough that merely acknowledging the pain doesn't heal the scars, though we certainly need to begin there. Doesn't it make better sense, in both humanitarian and economic terms, to stop the plague, especially since we know the cause? For child abuse is primarily perpetrated by men who lack, among other things, a basic empathy for others. Perpetrators get away with their crimes because society is structured to protect such men.

The most frightening thing about admitting that there is a problem is the potential that such an admission has for effecting change in our lives. Regardless how large or small the problem is, or whether that problem exists in one life or in society as a whole, as long as individuals cling to denial, things pretty much muddle along the way they always have, whether they are negative or even downright self-destructive. What we know is more comfortable than what we don't yet know and therefore fear. As long as society clings to denial, child abuse and violence against women serve to maintain the status quo, replicating patterns of abuse through the generations. If these issues are ever addressed with the sort of commitment they require, things are going to change. And this change, because it will affect the power distribution in society, is feared.

I believe child sexual abuse and violence against women are an integral structural part of patriarchal society and culture. They are how we — especially, but not only, women — are socialized to accept powerlessness. If this were any other issue with such a devastating effect, we'd have a massive mobilization of resources, we'd have comprehensive programmes, we'd have a blank cheque to enable us to do the work that needs to be done. If any other sort of plague or virus than the one called child abuse ravaged the children and left them crippled or destroyed, we'd find the resources to stop it. We'd immediately shift our attention from remote enemies in the oceans and skies and begin to deal effectively with an enemy closer to home. For if we do not have healthy children who have a reasonable chance of growing up to be healthy adults, we have nothing.

We urgently need to work to eradicate the privileges and abuses of power over others in society that makes every vulnerable person — child, woman, poor, disabled, disadvantaged, from a minority community, or old — a sitting duck or a victim. We need aggressive, effective and generously funded advocacy programmes to ensure that the rights of children are respected. We need to build communities in which the priority is the care, protection, nurturance, needs and rights of children and other vulnerable people. As the entire community becomes better sensitized to the needs of children, we will become more responsive to those of other disadvantaged people among us. And we will become a more generous, more cooperative and happier people. Then, and only then, will we be a truly healthy community.

Yes, what we must do is difficult, very difficult, but it is not impossible. Yes, there is help — for working together we can do anything. Yes, it can be done, if we allow ourselves to care enough. Each of us has an important contribution to make. All we have to do is begin. Today.

Epilogue

Turning fifty feels like a much more important marker on the road of life than turning thirty or forty did. Each decade has its own particular issues, tasks and joys. At thirty I wanted a home of my own; at forty I felt an urgency to deal with the baggage I was carrying from my past; as I approach fifty I feel it is time to have more fun, delight and joy in my life, to relax and be a little less serious — at least some of the time.

I feel physically and emotionally better than ever before. It seems like a time to make changes I've been postponing in the vain hope that I would someday be able to afford them. I think it is time to act and hope that it works out, whether there is money or not.

I also feel that I can now engage with my future in ways that were not possible before. I can make plans, set goals, go after my dreams, instead of merely wishing that things would change and all my dreams would magically come true.

There's a change of focus brought about by turning fifty; if important things are postponed much longer, there may not be time to do them at all. So there's a sense of urgency to the plans I'm making now. There are more books to write, and to make them possible I need to change my working environment to write them in health. My present universe feels too lonely, small and cramped, as though I'm root-bound and need more space to stretch and grow.

I want to live as part of a community, where new friendships are possible and where I can find a way to earn a living in the times between books. I'm not sure where I'm going to find what I want, but I'm determined to make a move in some positive direction as part of the celebrations of my fiftieth year.

Suggested Reading

Armstrong, Louise. *Rocking the Cradle of Sexual Politics: What Happened When Women Said Incest*. New York: Addison-Wesley, 1994.

Bass, Ellen and Laura Davis. *The Courage to Heal: A Guide for Women Survivors of Child Sexual Abuse*. New York: Harper Perennial Library, 1991.

Bell, Vikki. *Interrogating Incest: Feminism, Foucault, and the Law*. London: Routledge, 1993.

Bolen, Jean Shinoda. *Crossing to Avalon: A Woman's Midlife Pilgrimage*. San Francisco: HarperCollins, 1994.

Butler, Sandra. *Conspiracy of Silence: The Trauma of Incest*. Volcano, CA: Volcano, 1985.

Cameron, Julia. *The Artist's Way: A Spiritual Path to Higher Creativity*. New York: Tarcher/Perigree, 1992.

Carlson, Kathie. *In Her Image: The Unhealed Daughter's Search for Her Mother*. Boston: Shambhala, 1989.

Caruth, Cathy. *Unclaimed Experience: Trauma, Narrative and History*. Baltimore,

MD: John Hopkins University Press, 1996.

—. *Trauma: Explorations in Memory*. Baltimore, MD: John Hopkins University Press, 1995.

Davis, Laura. *Allies in Healing: When the Person You Love Was Sexually Abused as a Child, a Support Book*. New York: Harper Perennial Library, 1991.

—. *The Courage to Heal Workbook: For Women and Men Survivors of Child Sexual Abuse*. New York: HarperCollins, 1988.

Dueck, Lynnette. *Sing Me No More*. Vancouver: Press Gang, 1992.

Dworkin, Andrea. *Pornography: Men Possessing Women*. New York: Putnam, 1981.

—. *Woman Hating*. New York: Dutton, 1974.

"Family Secrets: Child Sexual Abuse." *Feminist Review* 28, Special Issue (Spring 1988), London, UK.

Forward, Susan and Craig Buck. *Betrayal of Innocence: Incest and Its Devastation*. New York: Penguin USA, 1988.

Gilbert, Lucy and Paula Webster. *Bound by Love: The Sweet Trap of Daughterhood*. Boston: Beacon, 1982.

Griffin, Susan. *Pornography and Silence: Culture's Revenge against Nature*. New York: Harper Colophon, 1982.

—. *Woman and Nature: The Roaring Inside Her*. New York: Harper Colophon, 1978.

Herman, Judith. *Trauma and Recovery: The Aftermath of Violence — From Domestic Abuse to Political Terror*. New York: Basic Books, 1992.

Hester, Marianne. *Lewd Women and Wicked Witches: A Study of the Dynamics of Male Domination*. New York: Routledge, 1992.

Kaminer, Wendy. *I'm Dysfunctional, You're Dysfunctional: The Recovery Movement and Other Self-Help Fashions*. New York: Addison-Wesley, 1992.

Kane, Evangeline. *Recovering from Incest: Imagination and the Healing Process*. Boston: Sigo, 1989.

Lee, Sharice A. *The Survivor's Guide: A Guide for Teenage Girls Who Are Survivors of Sexual Abuse*. Newbury Park, CA: Sage, 1995.

Leonard, Linda Schierse. *Witness to the Fire: Creativity and the Veil of Addiction*. Boston: Shambhala, 1990.

MacKinnon, Catharine. *Feminism Unmodified: Discourses on Life and Law*. Cambridge, MA: Harvard University Press, 1987.

Masson, Jeffrey Moussaieff. *Assault on Truth: Freud's Suppression of the Seduction Theory*. New York: Farrar, Straus and Giroux, 1984.

Meiselman, Karin C. *Resolving the Trauma of Incest: Reintegration Therapy with Survivors*. San Francisco: Jossey-Bass, 1990.

Miller, Alice. *Thou Shalt Not Be Aware: Society's Betrayal of the Child*. New York: New American Library, 1986.

—. *For Your Own Good: Hidden Cruelty in Child-Rearing and the Roots of Violence*. New York: Farrar, Straus and Giroux, 1984.

—. *The Drama of the Gifted Child: The Search for the True Self*. New York: Basic Books, 1981.

Morris, David B. *The Culture of Pain*. Berkeley: University of California Press, 1991.

Murdock, Maureen. *The Heroine's Journey*. Boston: Shambhala, 1990.

Prescott, Ellen. *Mondays Are Yellow, Sundays Are Grey: A Mother's Fight to Save Her Children from the Nightmare of Sexual Abuse*. Vancouver: Douglas & McIntyre, 1994.

Revoize, Jean. *Innocence Destroyed: A Study of Child Sexual Abuse*. New York: Routledge, 1993.

Rico, Gabriel. *Pain and Possibility: Writing Your Way through Personal Crisis*. Los Angeles: Tarcher, 1991.

Roberts, Julian V. and Renate M. Mohr. *Confronting Sexual Assault: A Decade of Legal and Social Change*. Toronto: University of Toronto Press, 1994.

Rush, Florence. *The Best Kept Secret: Sexual Abuse of Children*. New York: McGraw-Hill, 1980.

Russell, Diana. *The Secret Trauma: Incest in the Lives of Girls*. New York: Basic Books, 1986.

Scarry, Elaine. *The Body in Pain: The Making and Unmaking of the World*. New York: Oxford University Press, 1985.

Sher, Barbara. *Live the Life You Love*. New York: Delacorte, 1996.

—. *I Could Do Anything If I Only Knew What It Was*. New York: Delacorte, 1994.

Smart, Carol. *Regulating Womanhood: Historical Essays on Marriage, Motherhood, and Sexuality*. New York: Routledge, 1992.

Terr, Lenore. *Unchained Memories: True Stories of Traumatic Memories, Lost and Found*. New York, Basic Books, 1995.

—. *Too Scared to Cry: Psychic Trauma in Childhood*. New York: HarperCollins, 1992.

Ward, Elizabeth. *Father-Daughter Rape*. London: Women's Press (UK), 1984.

Whitfield, Charles L. *Memory and Abuse: Remembering and Healing the Wounds of Trauma*. Deerfield Beach, FL: Health Communications, 1995.

Author Information

The publication of *Don't: A Woman's Word* in 1988 cata-pulted Elly Danica to the lead-ing edge of the sexual abuse survivors movement. She has toured extensively in North America and Europe, given hundreds of lectures and in-terviews, and met thousands of survivors who touched her deeply with their stories. In the process she has gained public recognition and respect internationally.

DAVID SMILEY

Even today *Don't* has an undeniable impact on the way we, as a society, view child sexual abuse. The power and clarity of the writing in *Don't* have made it impossible to ignore the reality of child abuse. The skill with which this award-winning author has expressed her experience has earned her the admiration of many readers: from survivors to literary critics, from conference organizers to policy makers. Her long-awaited second book, *Beyond Don't: Dreaming Past the Dark*, is the continuation of Elly Danica's brave and inspiring story.

Elly Danica lives in an old church in Saskatchewan where she found sanctuary twenty years ago. There she continues to heal, write, paint and create her life. In 1996, she was awarded a year-long writer-in-residence position in a Saskatchewan community.

Elly Danica is available for lectures, workshops and consultations on topics related to recovery from child abuse and Life Writing. To contact Elly Danica, please write to her care of gynergy books or send e-mail to: e.danica@sk.sympatico.ca.

The Best of gynergy books

Across Borders: Women with Disabilities Working Together, *Diane Driedger, Irene Feika, Eileen Girón Batres (eds.).* This anthology combines personal stories with political activism in topical accounts from around the world. Multi-faceted partnerships between women with disabilities from developed and developing countries illustrate how women can learn from each other — across borders.
ISBN 0-921881-38-X $16.95/$14.95 U.S.

Each Small Step: Breaking the Chains of Abuse and Addiction, *Marilyn MacKinnon (ed.).* This groundbreaking anthology contains narratives by women recovering from the traumas of childhood sexual abuse and alcohol and chemical dependency.
ISBN 0-921881-17-7 $10.95

Imprinting Our Image: An International Anthology by Women with Disabilities, *Diane Driedger, Susan Gray (eds.).* "In this global tour de force, 30 writers from 17 countries provide dramatic insight into a wide range of issues germane to both the women's and the disability rights movements." *Disabled Peoples' International*
ISBN 0-921881-22-3 $12.95

Patient No More: The Politics of Breast Cancer, *Sharon Batt.* "A spectacular book ... carefully researched and thoroughly engrossing ... As exciting to read as a Grisham thriller, it demonstrates that reality is more compelling than fiction." *Bloomsbury Review*

Winner of the *1995 Laura Jamieson Award* for best feminist non-fiction book awarded by the Canadian Research Institute for the Advancement of Women (CRIAW).
ISBN 0-921881-30-4 $19.95/$16.95 U.S.

gynergy books titles are available at quality bookstores. Ask for our titles at your favourite local bookstore. Individual, prepaid orders may be sent to: gynergy books, P.O. Box 2023, Charlottetown, Prince Edward Island, Canada, C1A 7N7. Please add postage and handling ($3 for the first book and $1 for each additional book) to your order. Canadian residents add 7% GST to the total amount. GST registration number R104383120. Prices are subject to change without notice.